# The Professor's Obsessions

## Ruth Truman

*Enjoy!*
*Ruth Truman*

The Preservation Foundation, Inc.

Prologue

## No Safe College Review*

The Professor's Obsessions follows the children of the four main characters of No Safe College (2008*), in which Joan Reyes' daughter Jennie wants to attend Callegua University. Joan tells Jennie that first she must hear the story of her freshman year at Callegua. Then, if Jennie still wants to go to school there, Joan will agree.

Callegua is a religion based four-year school with an excellent reputation, the kind of school that makes parents feel that their teen-aged children are safe from the societal upheaval going on in the 1970's.

Joan is an innocent farm girl, the first one of her family to go to college. She expects the students and staff at Callegua to be like the people in her very conservative home church. Sue Pendella, sent to Callegua by her wealthy parents to save her from the drug and sex lifestyle she has adopted, is Joan's assigned roommate. Almost everything Sue does is a shock to Joan, but poor, timid and friendless, Joan allows herself to be drawn further and further into Sue's crowd of guys until an experience sends her screaming into a cold, snowy night, a night that turns her life around. Sue's freshman year ends with a betrayal by her boyfriend, J.W. Williams, and a dismissal from Callegua.

In the adjoining suite room is Trisha McClellan, who has come to Callegua because of its religious teaching and activities. She is, in the language of the 70's, on a Jesus Trip, equating every roommate problem as an opportunity to be set straight by prayer and a religious conversion experience. Ultimately, she helps Joan find a healthier group of friends.

Trisha shares the room with Angie, who rounds out the foursome. Focused on getting her education, she is beautiful in person and personality and frequently brings balance to the roommates' difficulties, but she falls in love and has sex with a senior resulting in an abortion only Joan knows about. In The Professor's Obsession, Jennie is a thriving sophomore in the 1990's at Callegua which has shifted to University status and a much more conservative theology.

* No Safe College is available at www.ruthtruman.com

### The Professor's Obsessions

### Jennie's Story:
### The 1990's

### 1.

Professor Benjamin Adkins saw her the moment he entered the lecture hall. For a moment he was breathless. Coughing to cover his momentary confusion, he strode to the lectern. The hall was full: his was a required class for graduation and underclassmen were trying to get it out of the way during their first two years of college. For most students history was a drag, so he tried to meet the requirements with a class in International Relationships of the 21st Century. Each semester he changed the class to focus on a different section of the world, and since Callegua was sponsoring an interim trip to Africa, he was focusing on Kenya. Realizing that the hall had grown quiet, he opened with his usual question: "Before we begin, do any of you have any questions about this course or its relevance to your future lives?"

*She* raised her hand. With his permission she asked, "Professor Adkins, will this class study the devastation of AIDS on interpersonal relationships in Africa?" Her voice was almost musical.

Ben suddenly felt off balance, unable to speak. After a long pause he found the words. "We will, in fact, be looking at the area around the orphanage begun by one of Callegua's graduates,

Trisha McClellan, that houses children affected by AIDS. Thank you for asking." With that he turned to the group, gave himself a reminder about the taboo on faculty/student relationships, and began the first lecture of the semester, glad to turn his attention away from the raven-haired beauty in the front row.

Dr. Ben, as the students called him, was one of the most popular teachers on campus. He was barely six years older than the sophomore students. An early high school graduate, his college was finished at twenty and his graduate degree at twenty-four. Coming to Callegua right from his doctoral program was a bit of a coup, allowing him to move into faculty housing and spend what little money he had on a yellow convertible that let him roar through the countryside when his pent-up emotions clamored for release. That was the way he was feeling this sunny September day as, classes over, he bounced along the gravel back roads.

The girl in his history class had upset him. He didn't even know her name, but he had this crazy notion that he wanted to marry her. He didn't want to marry anyone, he told himself. Life stretched out in endless adventure for him. Besides, he couldn't be involved with a student even if he wanted to. It would mean instant dismissal. His hiring committee had made that absolutely clear: no fraternizing with the students, period.

He turned into the parking lot of a diner, tucked back into the woods, a place he liked to come to unwind. His tall, tennis playing body unfolded itself to get out of the car, muscles rippling beneath his shirt. A lank of light brown hair had dropped over his high forehead, framing his deep blue eyes. Two other sets of eyes followed his entrance into the diner. Their owners called out, "Come on over, Ben. You look like you could use a beer!" Ben slid into the booth with Dr. John and Dr. Gene from the History Department. "What's the news today?" they queried.

"Same old, same old. Started my class today. And you guys?" was his response.

Dr. John looked cautiously around the diner, then leaned forward. In a low voice he announced, "They're going after the president!"

"Who....Clinton?"

"No, not him. The *college* president. He was seen a couple of towns south of here at an X-rated movie and somebody reported it to the Trustees. The word is they'll ask for his resignation." Dr. John sat back, tried to look troubled, but was triumphant that he had spread the gossip.

Ben moved his long frame uncomfortably, thinking of the girl in his class. "For a movie? They'd replace him for that?" he said incredulously. "Surely the trustees aren't that narrow minded, right?"

Dr. Gene nodded his head in the affirmative. "The last one went because he wasn't properly dressed when a wealthy donor showed up unannounced. She took offense, and had him fired!"

Gene had been in on that one, had sat on the faculty investigating committee, and tried his best to protect the president who was really very good for Callegua. The current one had lasted just two years. Of course, that was about how long college presidents were staying these days. Dr. Gene planned to keep his nose clean and lie low until he got tenure. He had another year to go.

Ben studied his two friends. Could he trust them for advice? There wasn't anyone else he could talk to, so he plunged in: "Have either of you guys dated a student? I mean, I haven't, but I've got a girl in one of my classes that really attracts me and I'd like to get to know her. What do you say?"

Both John and Gene threw up their hands in mock horror. "Depart from us, you worker of iniquity! We never knew you!"

Dr. John chuckled. Yes, he had been there, seen a beautiful girl—and made her his wife. But that was in grad school, not when he was a teacher at Callegua. Dr. Gene was the one to answer. "Run like hell, Ben. One date and you're out of here. You know that."

"But isn't there a way to get acquainted without crossing that line?" Ben persisted. "I'm really attracted, but I don't even know her name."

"Pretend her name is Out-of-Here, so every time you see her it will remind you that you're playing with fire," shot back Dr. John. He liked Ben, a good friend, but he'd seen better men than him come and go at Callegua because they broke the fraternization rule. "OK, OK. I hear you loud and clear." Then, wanting to change the subject, added, "So do you really think they'll dump the president?"

The waitress came by the booth and the three of them ordered a burger and a beer. At Callegua, even the beer could cast suspicion on their careers, but they were safe at the diner. It was a couple of hours and lots of laughter before the three of them left. To Ben's relief, the subject of "the girl" never came up again.

**2.**

"Mother? I've got great news. I've been chosen to lead the university's Interim mission team to Kenya. We're going to work at the orphanage your roommate Trisha created. But I have to have your permission. And I have to pay half my cost.

Can we do that?"

"Jennie, I'm so proud of you for being chosen, and of course I will let you go, " her mother replied, "but I'll have to check my books to see if we can afford it. Send me the details of the trip as soon as you can."

"Is your business going okay? I mean, if this is a burden, I'll just tell the Dean to get someone else."

"No, just call me tomorrow and I'll give you an answer."

Jennie clicked off her cell phone. Money. I thought mother had plenty. We've never discussed it. And Spring tuition has to be paid right after Interim. I love Callegua. It's everything I hoped it would be: vibrant, a tough, faculty, tough enough for anyone wanting to be a doctor like me. I wonder if mother felt this way when she was here in the 70's? Once she got past her tough freshman year she loved this school, graduated with honors, was even elected to Who's Who in American Colleges and Universities. Only a few students received that honor and her mother was one of them!

Gathering up her books, she headed across campus to her chemistry class.

Meanwhile Jennie's mother, Joan, was mulling over the cost of keeping Jennie in Callegua. It was financially tough, but so far she had been able to make enough profit from her agricultural business to pay the bills. Now Jennie wanted to go to Kenya at Interim. Joan wasn't sure where she would get the money. Times were good, but her profit margin was always narrow. And what if Jennie decided to stay in Africa? Trisha could be quite persuasive, even manipulative. She had maneuvered Joan into fellowship at Callegua, hadn't she? Even if it turned out to be a good thing....

And Jennie was all the family she had. Jennie was smart and totally unaware of the effect she had on other people. When she was elected homecoming queen in her senior year of high school, she had been amazed. Her skin was flawless, her black hair accented her dark eyes, and at 5'8" Jennie was just tall and slender enough to look good in anything she wore, yet clothes were unimportant to her. She was a great combination of her father's Hispanic roots and her own Irish background. Joan admitted to herself that sometimes she was envious of Jennie's beauty. Next to her, she thought, I'm really a "plain Jane". But Jennie had proven herself trustworthy in her first year. Jennie loved Callegua. She even liked the rules, the required chapel attendance. And her grades were terrific. If she wanted to go into medicine as she said, grades would not be a problem. Money might be, however. Med school was not cheap.

"Of course I'll find the money," Joan said aloud, her voice affirming what her mind was thinking. "Of course she must go. I've invested my life in Jennie and this is not the time to hold her back." Africa at Interim it was. Her letter went out in the mail that afternoon, signed, 'Love always, Mother.'

**3.**

"Jennie, wait up!"

The call brought a smile to Jennie's face as she turned to wait for Meghan. Meeting Meghan, a sparkling blue-eyed, blonde freshman, was exciting to her. For Meghan the campus and college were all new, and Jennie enjoyed watching her. Probably they would become life-long friends. They had discovered that their mothers had been suite mates in the 70's and later had been in each other's weddings!

"Where are you headed?"

"On my way to English Lit. How about you?

"Chemistry, I'm afraid. Not my favorite."

Meghan's face told her what she thought of Chemistry, making Jennie laugh.

"Well I can't get into Med School without Chemistry, Meghan. So I'm getting it out of the way in my Sophomore year. If I can I'd like to skip my senior year and go straight to med study after next year."

"Really? Can you do that? I'll have to take five years to be an elementary teacher, and you only have to go three to be a doctor?"

"Not quite. It will take about seven more to be called 'doctor'. By the way, have I told you about my mother's freshman year here? Wow, was Callegua ever different then."

"How? Wasn't it a Christian school just like now?"

"Yes, but it was the '70's, and college students everywhere demanded freedom from rules; they were using drugs, alcohol, all that stuff. My mother was right off the farm and totally naive. She was assigned to a four-girl suite with Sue, a roommate from UC Berkeley. Sue's parents sent her to Callegua to get her away from drugs and sex, but they were too late. She was the total opposite of my mom, got her into real trouble because she was so innocent."

"What about the other girls? Didn't they help your mom?"

"They tried. But she got scared straight one night, sort of grew up right then, and got herself turned around. She turned into an honor student after that."

"And her roommates?"

"Sue was caught stealing exam papers, almost committed suicide, and was put out of Callegua. Trisha helped Mom get into the right groups: she's the one who founded the orphanage we're going to in Kenya. And the fourth girl, Angie, fell in love her freshman year, got pregnant, and had an abortion because her guy was a senior and a baby didn't fit with his career plans. They got married, though, and she finished college."

"Really? An abortion? I've been thinking about starting a Right To Life Club on campus, but I wasn't sure it was needed at Callegua. I guess I was wrong. Maybe I'll do it."

The girls came to a divide in the walkway.

"Here's the Science Building. How about meeting me for lunch?"

"Wait, Jennie. What did you say the name was of the girl who had the abortion?"

"Angie."

"Jennie, my mother's name is Angie. Do you suppose...." Meghan's voice trailed off.

"We'll talk at lunch, Meghan. I wouldn't worry about it. See you then." With that Jennie disappeared into the Science Building.

## 4.

Meghan had plunged into campus life almost as soon as she arrived. Petite, a born leader, she had quickly made friends by trying out several clubs to see which she wanted to belong to. A straight-A student in high school with good study habits, she had plenty of time for extra-curricular activities. Politics enticed her, and it was easy to notice that one of the hottest topics, the right to life, was going untended on campus, so even before she talked to Jennie she had decided to start a club devoted to making students aware of the need to fight abortion. She could hardly contain herself after Jennie told her their mothers' stories. Here she was about to start a Right-to-Life Club on campus and she had just learned that her mother had had an abortion. Why didn't she know this? As soon Lit class was over, Meghan sat down at her computer and fired off an angry email to her parents, Ron and Angie.

Angie and Ron Kronen were both graduates of Callegua and were happy that their only daughter had chosen their alma mater for her college education. They trusted the institution and felt Meghan would gain both a good education and a happy experience. All the emails and phone calls had confirmed their hopes so far, but now Angie stared at the computer screen in disbelief. The email from Meghan contained the secret she and Ron had carefully kept all these years. How would she answer her daughter? How could she explain? It was so long ago, so right at the time.

Not that she hadn't thought of the unborn child almost every day. What would it have looked like? Was it a boy or a girl? Would she and Ron have managed if they had married right away? That their daughter would meet Joan's daughter, Jennie, at Callegua was so improbable, but it had happened. She hadn't heard from Joan in years, not since Joan's husband Jim had died. She didn't even know that Jennie was at Callegua, for that matter. And Joan had told Jennie the whole story, about Sue and her attempted suicide, all the drugs and sex that happened in the 70's. Then Jennie had told Meghan.

Angie sat motionless, reading the email over and over. She and Ron had vowed to keep the college abortion secret for life. After all, it was different with her and Ron back then. They knew right away they would marry; they just needed to get on their feet before children entered their lives.

They should have waited, but they didn't. And now her daughter wanted to know why her mother, her very own mother, had an abortion. Meghan wanted to know why she *murdered* not just a child, but her brother or sister?

Maybe Ron would help her with the right answer. After all, how could she explain the 70's to Meghan; conservative Meghan; right-to-life Meghan; virginity-pledged Meghan?

Angie signed out of her email. She would answer it later....

## 5.

In Chicago, Sue Williams, Joan, Trisha, and Angie's other suite mate from the 70's, had long since forgiven J.W for his cruelty toward her in her freshman year. She had even married him. He had become a very successful businessman and they lived well. Between the inheritance from her mother, the constant gifts from her father, her Callegua lawsuit, and J.W.'s income, there was always plenty of money. Her closets were full of designer clothes. Their home was decorated by one of the finest home decorators in Chicago and was included almost every year in the Christmas tour put on by the Women's Club. But Sue was restless, even though she enjoyed her place as a sought-out society matron. Their son Doug and daughter Laina had moved away: Laina to California to try breaking into film and TV, and Doug to Florida, working in the tourist trade. Neither of them was married and there were no grandchildren, so she rarely felt the need to visit them.

Now Doug had offered her a disturbing proposition. He was doing the travel arrangements for a Kenya trip to take place during interim break at Callegua University. They would go to the orphanage founded by Trisha McClellan, the "Jesus

Trip" girl who lived in the other half of her suite in college who was always trying to 'save' her. The purpose of the trip was to let the students see firsthand the situation of the AIDS orphans. Sue didn't want to be confronted by sickness and poverty, nor Trisha, for that matter. She liked life just the way it was. And why was Doug doing business with Callegua anyway? He was in Florida, not the Midwest. This trip put a bad taste in her mouth....

In Kenya, Trisha was anxiously awaiting Doug William's email. She marveled that in the heart of Africa she could communicate so easily. Having Callegua students visit the orphanage had long been her dream and now, finally, it was about to come true. From her desk at the front of the bare classroom she watched as her students bent over their desks, carefully printing their assignment to write about family members who had died of AIDS. Trisha wanted their stories written down so that when the Callegua students arrived they could quickly familiarize themselves with what the children had faced in their young lives. Had anyone been looking, the woman at the desk had a face etched with love, topped by graying hair pulled back in a pony tail, whose clothes were as worn as those of her students. Trisha seldom spent anything on herself, so great was her desire to enrich the lives of the impoverished children, and once her hair was combed in the morning, she never glanced in the mirror again that day.

She was grateful to her church in America for helping to build this school and sending money that allowed her to feed the children one good meal a day. These were the children she never had. God had given them to her to put love in her life when she heard God's call to mission. She had come to

Africa alone after getting her master's degree in education and studying Swahili and French. Never had she thought she would remain unmarried. At first it was very hard to be alone, but the work had consumed her. She was changing lives for Christ and that had become enough. And now the Callegua students would come to make a huge difference in "her children's" lives. She could hardly wait.

## 6.

Jennie was officially named the contact for the Kenya trip. The Dean of Students gave her a small workspace with a computer and phone so she could receive information from Doug Williams in Florida and then forward his email to all the students who were registered to go. So far there were eighteen, including the Student Body President, Samuel Katata, a Kenyan attending Callegua as a foreign student. He had been holding seminars for the participants, teaching them some Swahili. He said most adults spoke English for business, but the children might not know it. Trisha, who ran the orphanage, had sent pictures of the children in class, on the play yard, and individual pictures with each child's name. In a few days she would send their stories so the group could get to know their backgrounds. It was all very exciting to Jennie. And thanks to her mother, she was able to go.

She was in her workspace when she heard a familiar voice. A little *too* familiar voice. It seemed everywhere she went her history professor would appear. He was always reserved and polite, like now as he looked over her shoulder at the computer screen. "How's it going?" queried Ben Adkins, hoping his voice was casual. "Looks like the trip is coming together, right?"

"Yes, thank you," was Jennie's cool reply.
"But if you'll excuse me, I don't have time to chat.
I have to get these messages out and I only have a
half hour till my next class." She kept her eyes on
the screen.

"Oh, sorry," Ben responded, backing away
from Jennie. At least he knew her name now:
Jennie Reyes. He had checked on her home address
and found she lived in Iowa, probably on a farm
since the address had a route number and a small-
town name. A nineteen-year-old sophomore, her
declared major was pre-med, and so far she was a
straight A student. Only her mother's name was on
her record, so her parents were either divorced or
her father was deceased. It was amazing what could
be found from a simple college application and
transcript record.

Jennie had already forgotten him in her
concentration on the task. She took Doug's
message about visas and inoculations, flights, etc.,
modified it and sent it out to the group. She loved
computers. They fit her scientific, logical mind
perfectly. Since only she and Samuel had access to
this computer, she shut it down for the day, grabbed
her backpack, and headed out to her calculus class.
As she went out the door she saw that Professor
Adkins was standing just a few feet away. She
turned around, went back inside, and left by another
door.

Ben watched her retreat and gave himself the
now familiar lecture to stay away from her. But she
fascinated him. All he wanted to do was get
acquainted so he could discover that he really
*wouldn't* like her if he got to know her. He was
trying to be discreet, keeping his distance in places
where he might be observed, but using small
opportunities to approach her without suspicion that

he was fraternizing with a student. She certainly had not shown any sign of wanting to be friends. If anything, she gave him the cold shoulder every time he spoke to her.

In class, Jennie concentrated on the calculus problems on the white board. So far she was staying on course with her studies so that even calculus seemed simple. One glance around the room showed that several other students were struggling to understand the problems, so her mind took a short vacation while the professor explained the work again. Ben Adkins was becoming a nuisance. He had just happened to sit at her table in the dining room two days ago and was two rows behind her at the football game last Saturday. Today it looked like he was waiting to walk with her to this class. She snapped back to attention as the class moved on to the next set of problems. It was probably just her imagination.

Meghan was waiting for her after class to go to lunch. Jennie liked Meghan, though sometimes she got a little bit too radical for comfort. She could see that Meghan was really excited.

"Jennie, Jennie! It's just the greatest! I got permission to start the Right To Life club! It's for pro-life people. Will you help me get out some publicity? You're so good at that." Meghan had rattled her news so fast Jennie could scarcely understand her.

"Slow down, Meghan. You'll have a stroke. Let's get some food in us and then we'll talk," said a calm Jennie.

After they had picked up their trays in the cafeteria, the two girls found a quiet spot off to themselves where they could talk uninterrupted. They were silent for a few minutes while they took the edge off their hunger. Finally the talkative Meghan could stand it no longer and blurted out,

"Jennie, you know how you told me my mom had an abortion when she was in college? Do you realize that's the sister or brother I never had? I was cheated out of family just because they were afraid they would hurt dad's career! Can you imagine anything worse?"

Jennie could think of many worse things, but she just nodded her head to encourage Meghan to continue. If this helped her get rid of anger, then Jennie figured she could listen.

"I mean, can you believe that my mother and dad had sex before they were married? Why couldn't they wait like they expect me to? My dad was so big into this thing about being a virgin, had me wear this ring and everything as a promise." Meghan paused to look at her ring, then pulled it off and rolled it onto the table where Jennie caught it before it fell on the floor.
"I don't believe such hypocrisy!" Meghan was fairly boiling with anger. "That's why I'm going to make sure no one else ends up like me, an only child with one unborn, dead sibling. So as of today I'm starting the club. We'll spread the word how terrible it is to take a child's life. No baby should be dumped down the drain! You will help me with publicity, won't you?"

Jennie thought of the things she had seen during last summer's internship. It was in a poor neighborhood of Des Moines where women couldn't afford any maternity care except at Planned Parenthood clinics. She had witnessed three abortions, each very early term, two of which were by married women who simply had no resources to care for another child. The third mother was infected with cancer and with no man to help her she was choosing between her life and the unborn fetus, plus staying alive to care for the two small children she already had. This was the kind of decision Jennie knew she would have to face as a doctor. Meghan was only looking on the surface when she championed every child carried to full term. But there was no reason to argue with Meghan. Nor explain. Meghan's hearing was dulled by anger.

"I'm glad for you, Meghan. You will no doubt help a lot of students clarify their thinking and that's good. And yes, I'll do some flyers for you or whatever. You have to do the design work, though. I just don't have time, what with pulling the Kenya trip together."

Meghan, always a little flighty, jumped on the new subject. "You are so lucky to go, Jennie! I wish I could—well to be honest, I don't really want to go. Unfamiliar places give me the creeps. It was hard enough just coming to college. I can't imagine what it would be like to go into another country, especially if I couldn't speak English to everyone. I think the whole world should speak English, don't you?" Without waiting for an answer, she continued, "Aren't you afraid? I mean there's AIDS and the mosquitoes that carry those weird fevers, and you probably won't have any privacy and have to eat strange food. I hear they even eat bugs and things. That is so gross!"

Jennie just smiled at Meghan. She was young, just seventeen, and she had a lot to learn. Though Jennie's mother and she had never resorted to eating bugs, they had eaten just about everything else when they were struggling after her dad died. And she knew that AIDS wasn't 'catching', and the inoculations would protect her from all the major diseases. Sure, there was a chance of some primitive virus breaking out in Kenya, but it wasn't likely in the four weeks the group would be there.

As the girls made their way across the dining hall to deposit their trays at the dishwashing counter, they stopped to chat with various friends until Meghan, still high with enthusiasm for her new project, said goodbye to Jennie and settled herself at a new table, talking nonstop. Jennie smiled to herself as she dropped off her dishes; Meghan was really quite a kick, a fun, good friend. It was in this happy mood that her way was suddenly blocked by her history professor saying, "Jennie, can we talk? I want to discuss that paper you turned in yesterday."

Irritated, but under the circumstances helpless, Jennie turned aside with Dr. Adkins to the student lounge. The only seating available was a couch, part of a square of couches in the center of the room. So far as Jennie was concerned, he sat too close to her so that when he showed her the paper, the pillows caved in toward each other and their shoulders touched. The paper was covered with a sheet of comments he had written, and he began to go over each one.

Bright enough to recognize trivia when she saw it, Jennie's irritation rose. If he had wanted to talk to her he could have invited her to his office, could have made an appointment, and she found herself saying this aloud.

"Of course," apologized Dr. Adkins, "that was thoughtless of me. Can you come tomorrow about three?" He moved away slightly, closed the paper, and pulled out his schedule book. This was working better than he had hoped: she would come to his office. Why hadn't he thought of simply making an appointment to discuss the paper?

Jennie pulled out her own schedule, saw she had nothing at 3 p.m. the next day, and grudgingly agreed. As they were saying goodbye, Meghan came along and Jennie gratefully fell into step with her, scarcely hearing Meghan as she babbled on, "Oooh, he is so good looking. And single. What a catch! Maybe he likes you, Jennie. Don't you agree?"

A dark shadow crossed Jennie's face. "No, I don't agree. He is a professor and that's all. And he's beginning to bother me, showing up in too many places. I wish he'd leave me alone! And I think I'll tell him so tomorrow when I go to his office to discuss my paper."

"Well, I'd love for him to pay attention to me," Meghan said. "I think he's drooley cool."

"He's all yours, Meghan. I don't have time for romance. I'll be in school for a long time—the rest of Callegua and med school. So go for it, girl! I'll cheer from the sidelines."

Laughing, the two girls headed for their separate rooms and soon both were buried in their studies. Midterms were coming up fast and Jennie was determined to keep her perfect GPA.

Dr. Ben waited anxiously for Jennie the next day. When she arrived promptly at three, he indicated a chair next to his desk and turned away, lest she see the flush in his cheeks. Being this close to her was almost more than he could handle. Quickly he picked up the paper they were to discuss, laid it down on the desk beside her, and began a steady stream of questions about its content. He had to make sure it was her original work, not copied from any source, and that all her "facts" were correct. Jennie was curious about his questioning, but not wanting to stay even one second longer than she had to, she held her conversation strictly to her responses. At last he seemed satisfied that the paper stood up well with just a few revisions, which she agreed to make by the following day. Why he was so concerned about this simple history paper was beyond her, but if the revisions got him away from her, she would be sure they were done ASAP.

As Jennie left the office she noticed pictures of Dr. Ben windsurfing and playing tennis. A tennis trophy sat on top of his bookcase. Normally Jennie's curiosity would have made her ask about these things, but not today, not from Dr. Ben. The less she knew about him the better. Within the hour she was in her room at her computer; by dinner time the last page was coming out of her printer and she had a plan: She would slide the revisions under the door of his office at 8:15 tomorrow morning, while he was gone, teaching his first class. Had anyone been around to hear, they would have heard her chuckle to herself as she headed out to the library.

## 7.

The semester went on, and Meghan's mother, Angie, began to dread Thanksgiving. Meghan would be home and Angie couldn't put off explaining to her why she had an abortion when she was in college. She knew Meghan was angry. Very angry. On the rare occasion that she had called, her words were sharp and brief. The loving daughter had disappeared. Angie felt like she was having a second abortion, only this time the baby was 17 years old. Ron was completely bewildered by Meghan's attitude and Angie hadn't had the courage to tell him what the problem was. After all, he was the one who had insisted she get rid of the baby because it might mess up his future career. A flash of anger went through Angie. She had never made him take responsibility for his part. She didn't get pregnant by herself. In fact, she was the one who wanted to wait until they were married, but he kept insisting. Even the college counselor wasn't much help; all that talk about the spirit entering the baby after it was born. Angie knew now that was the rationalization that allowed the counselor to send the girls off for abortions. How many had there been? Probably a lot more than anyone knew, since no one talked about it.

At dinner, Ron studied his wife's expression. "You're awfully quiet tonight, Angie. What's up?" He smiled, still amazed that he had married this wonderful, talented woman. What a help she had been to his career, and then had struck out on her own to develop her own business. He was so proud of her, so proud to have her in his life. "Another phone call from Meghan?" "No. No. I'm just dreading Thanksgiving this year. Meghan expects us to sit down and explain…." Angie averted her eyes. She couldn't look at Ron. After all these years she was still filled with guilt.

"Explain what?" was Ron's innocent question.

"The abortion." There. It was out.

"The abortion? You told her? Why did you do that? We pledged to keep it a life secret." Ron's voice was rising. "Angie, I can't believe you would betray us like that!"

"But I didn't. I didn't.

"Then who? Who else would know?"

"Do you remember my college roommate, Joan? She took me to the hospital, so she knew, too. Apparently her daughter and our daughter have become friends at Callegua, and Joan had told her daughter Jennie the whole story of our freshman year. Then Jennie innocently asked Meghan if we had ever talked about it. That's how Meghan knows." Angie was trembling inside. Only one other time had she seen Ron's temper and it frightened her then; it frightened her now.

Ron pushed back his chair from the table, threw down his napkin, and jerked to his feet. "So I suppose the whole college will know. Meghan is just angry enough to do that to us. And then it will follow her home and the church will know. For God's sake, Angie, I'm an Elder. This won't go down well." He picked up his chair and banged it on the floor, shattering the peace of their quiet suburban home. Shaking, he pointed his finger at Angie. "Well, you're the one who had the abortion! Not me. It was your responsibility to make sure you didn't get pregnant, but you didn't, did you? You were all sweet and honey, making me crazy with wanting you, and then you didn't keep your part of the bargain. That baby has been a thorn in our relationship forever!" He whirled around, stomped out through the back door, and slammed it behind him.

Angie sat, stunned. Ron had accused her totally, had disclaimed any action on his part. Neither of them had used birth control; she knew that. They thought if they didn't have sex very often everything would be fine. He didn't know she had been to the counselor before they started. If only she had taken the counselor's advice. But she didn't. She loved Ron too much to turn him down. And now, after all these years, he had turned on her. And so, thought Angie, had her daughter.

When Ron returned to the house later that night, his only words to Angie were "I hope you've got it all figured out. Some Thanksgiving this will be!"

When they went to bed he turned his back to her and there was no goodnight kiss.

## 8.

Doug Williams had inherited his entrepreneurial spirit from his dad, J.W. Doug's Florida travel agency had many clients, but he was especially intrigued by the Callegua University interim trip to Kenya. An announcement in the school alumni newsletter caught his eye when he had visited his parents the previous summer, so he had called the administration to see if he could help with the travel arrangements. His mother wasn't exactly an alumnus, he knew she had only gone there one year, but his father was still remembered for his football prowess. And now that he was wealthy there were constant requests for money, so the college was eager to pass their travel business along to a wealthy alumni's son. Doug thought about his last conversation with his dad concerning the money he kept sending to Callegua.

"Well, son, Callegua was pretty good to me; pulled me through in a crunch once in my junior year, so I guess I owe them a little help in return. It's not enough to affect your inheritance, if that's what you're wondering about. Plenty to go around for that. No. I just like knowing some young football player will do well because I put up money for a scholarship or two. Your mother's not too keen on it, though, so I don't talk to her about it. She probably wouldn't want me to send them a penny! And you shouldn't talk to her about it either."

As Doug brought up the Kenya trip details on his office computer, he wondered idly why his parents had such different views of Callegua U. His mother certainly didn't want him to go there, and since he didn't play football, or any sports for that matter, his father agreed that some other college might be better. Neither of them had figured on his living at home and going to community college. Living at home had sure helped his finances! He chuckled as he thought how shocked they had been when he showed up with a Porsche 911e, paid for. A used one, of course, but he hadn't stayed at home for nothing. He had saved almost all his earnings from the odd jobs he had worked those two years of college. It was Spring Break when he came down to Florida and picked up an invitation to join a travel agency, and what with so many older residents who liked to travel, he was doing well. A couple more years and he figured on buying a *new* Porsche.

Meantime he had work to do. His contact at Callegua was awaiting his email. Doug scanned the computer screen to find her name: ah, there it was. Jennie. Jennie Reyes. That sounded like a Hispanic name. He envisioned a dark eyed, dark-haired beauty and decided maybe he should accompany the Callegua group. It could be very interesting....

Moments later he was sending information on visas, passports, and inoculations, making a mental note to upgrade his shots as well, just in case he decided to go to Kenya. Another email went to his mother, encouraging her again to go with the Callegua group as a chaperone. It would be good for her to find a new interest. And a third email went to Trisha who sounded like someone his mother would like to know, plus his mother had plenty of money available to help with the orphanage. Actually she had lots of money from some old lawsuit, something she seldom talked about. All Doug knew was that it involved Callegua some way. Some day he should ask her about it. After all, that might be part of his inheritance too. Maybe his sister Laina knew something.

The important work done, Doug glanced at the clock: ten. California time was three hours earlier than Florida, so Laina would still be home. He picked up the phone. "Hey, sis! How're you doing? Yeah, Doug here." His hand automatically reached for a pencil as he began to doodle, listening to his sister's account of her latest auditions, only vaguely registering that she was a finalist for a TV series part. "That's great, kid. When you're rich and famous I hope you'll still speak to me. Hey, I'm trying to get Mom to go to Kenya with the Callegua University group and I got to wondering, thought maybe you'd know where Mom got her money. Some lawsuit or something. Know anything about it?"

Doug grabbed another piece of paper and began to make notes as fast as he could. He could barely believe what he was hearing. His mom and dad had been called up before the disciplinary council for stealing tests and papers. His dad had laid all the blame on his mom and had walked free. She was kicked out of the school and tried to commit suicide. Drugs. Alcohol. Sex. His sister knew the whole story. "Why the hell didn't they ever tell me?" he asked Laina. "Yeah, you're probably right. I wouldn't have believed it 'cause I idolize Dad so. Wow! This is really a shocker! No wonder Mom never wanted to go back to campus. But I still don't understand where the money came from."

Laina glanced at the clock. She was due at the studio in twenty minutes and didn't have time for this conversation right now. "She sued Callegua for dismissing her without proof of the allegations, and rather than have a big story get out to the public, they paid her off. Half a mil—a lot of money in the 70's—and she invested it well. That's all I can tell you right now. Sorry, I gotta go. Wish me luck!"

"Thanks, sis. Break a leg. Be sure and let me know how it turns out, ok?" The last sentence was spoken into a dead phone. Laina was already out the door.

Doug read through his notes slowly, trying to absorb what he had written, what his sister had said. These were his parents? Stealing tests? Sex orgies? Drugs? Alcohol to loosen up the girls, his mother?

The almost perfect people who had raised him and his sister? If it was so, and he knew it must be, why did they get married? If his dad dumped the blame on his mother, why would she even speak to him ever again?

He picked up the phone again, but this time it was his mother he wanted to talk to. The answering machine took the call at the other end. He quietly hung up the phone. Maybe it was just as well no one was home. He really needed to think about this.

Later, on the road, watching the sun dip over the ocean, Doug pulled out his cell phone. "Mom. Good to talk to you. I wanted to ask you …." He couldn't bring himself to say it. "I wanted to ask you if you've thought anymore about going to Kenya? I need to line up your visas and flights and the earlier we do that the better." He was glad to have her cut the call short because someone was at her door. After all, this was his mother. Did he really want to know what she had done in college? It was a long time ago and whatever happened, she had straightened out her life, had made peace with his dad, and was living a good life. Sometimes it was best just to let things be, and this was one of those times. But $500 grand! It must have been really bad for the school to want to cover it up that much. It also meant that by now the money had probably grown to a couple mil. His inheritance looked better all the time. Of course, his folks were young. It would be a long time before he inherited anything, but nice to know that if his own efforts didn't pay off, there would still be money to count on. He wheeled into the carport, grabbed the take-out he had picked up on the way home, and settled in for a comfortable evening in front of the TV.

He was asleep on the couch when the Hollywood gossip program came on, so he missed

the word that Laina Williams had been cast in
Rose's Place, the top running show that year.

## 9.

Samuel Katata's black skin glistened in the
October sun. A tall, muscular man, he was at
Callegua because of a missionary alumnus who had
come to his village in Kenya. Samuel had heard the
message of a God of love, so different from what
his people worshiped, and had decided to be a
Christian. At first his wife Zaporra was unhappy
with his decision because it made them outsiders,
targets of mocking by their village and people
whom they had known all their lives. But eventually
she realized how different he was in his actions
toward her and the children and she too became a
convert.

Every morning they would begin their day
with prayer, and over each meal their children, Paul
and Lydia, would try to pray a thank you for the
food. Samuel smiled as he remembered Paul
struggling to say "Dear God, Thank you for our
food. Amen." They were indeed grateful for the
food since it was often scarce and sometimes the
government handouts were all they had to eat.

Watching the rising violence in the villages,
Samuel felt called to teach others about the love of
Christ and His forgiveness, even though he often
met resistance from his neighbors and friends. They
warned him that he could be in danger if the radical
guerrillas came to their village. Nevertheless, he
sought out the missionary he had first met who
suggested he should go to school to learn more
about the Bible before he became a pastor. Since
there were no training schools available in Kenya,
the missionary arranged for Samuel to go to

Callegua on full scholarship.

This was a wrenching decision for Samuel and his wife. He had to leave the family for four years because there was no money for him to travel back and forth. He spent almost a year in preparation courses before he could begin his actual college class work. At Callegua he enrolled in summer schools, during the school year took extra credits in order to finish sooner, and worked on campus to pay for extra costs. Out of this money he managed to send a small amount back to his wife and children in Kenya. And now, with nine months to go until he graduated, the interim trip to Kenya was going to allow him to be with his family for a whole month!

Being a Christian had turned him into a happy, outgoing sort of person; but these days the joy in his heart expressed itself in his brilliant smile, making him more popular on campus than he already was. His Kenyan seminars with the students who were going on the trip thrilled him to his soul. He loved his country, and as happy as he had been at Callegua, he couldn't wait to be back with his family in his own village. He would be thirty by the time he finished college, which seemed so old until he reminded himself that Christ had begun his ministry at thirty. Not a bad example.

Samuel checked his post box outside the dorm this glad October day Quickly he scanned the letter from his wife:

> Dearest Sammie,
> I want you to know that the children and I are able to come to the orphanage while the Callegua group is there. The missionaries have provided money to help pay our way. It might help us buy rides along the

road. Otherwise we will walk and
sleep alongside the road. The
children will think it is a great
adventure. They are anxious to see
you, as am I! I hope you will not
think I am too much older than when
we parted three years ago. It seems
like ten years—or more. But soon we
will be together again and I can rest
in your powerful arms. I can scarcely
wait. Maybe January will come early
this year! Please always love me, as
I surely do love you. Come soon.
Zaporra

He feared for her safety no matter how brave
she sounded in her letter. He would write her
tonight and urge her to have a neighbor travel with
her. How glad he would be when she arrived safely.
And the children. He hoped this would not be too
great a trip for them and they would not be too
afraid. They wouldn't know him, of course. The
oldest was four and the baby not quite one when he
left, so neither of them would remember him. Was
college worth it? Absolutely. He would do it all
over again. But he was oh, so glad to get to be with
his wife, even if only for a month.

## 10.

Samuel's large body filled the small interim
trip office space. Jennie was not there, but she had
left notes for him from several of the participants.
On top was a note about Doug Williams, their travel
agent, saying that he and possibly his mother Sue
would be going with them. Doug was going out of
curiosity and his mother, who had once been a
Callegua student, had consented to be a chaperone.

Samuel sat down at the computer, sent a reply to Doug thanking him for his help, and then casually brought up the alumni files. Sue Williams was not there, just J.W. Williams. He knew from previous conversations with Doug that J.W. was his father and noted that Doug had said his mother had been a student at Callegua, so Samuel supposed that meant she had not graduated and therefore was not on the alumni list. Just then Jennie arrived.

"Hi, Samuel, how are you doing?" was Jennie's greeting.

"Thank you, fine," he responded, adding, "Do you know anything about Sue Williams? Doug says she'll go along as a chaperone."

Jennie burst out laughing, remembering her mother's story about Sue. "A chaperone? That's a good one! My mother roomed with her most of her freshman year and I know a lot about her. But I suppose she's changed. She was quite a rounder, even got kicked out of college." No need to say why, Jennie thought. Sue might be a perfectly great person now.

"Well, is she a Christian? We don't want any bad influences on the group or the children." Samuel's voice was edged with concern.

"I couldn't really say. Guess you'll have to ask Doug. I've never met her. She's probably just fine, and we could use another adult along. You know the youngest one going is just seventeen, and you never know how people will act when they get out of their familiar surroundings." Meghan's conversation a few days before popped into Jennie's mind, about how creepy it would be in another country. Neither Samuel nor Jennie were well acquainted with everyone in the group, so they had to be prepared for anything. Then Jennie added, "Have you heard from your wife?"

Samuel smiled broadly and patted the letter that stuck out of his shirt pocket. "Today. She is coming. And the children. But pray for her safety. She must walk or catch rides, and sleep by the road. It frightens me."

"Time to trust God, Samuel. You're always telling us that. Now it's your turn." Jennie seldom spoke of God or her faith. Her answer surprised her, even though deep down she was a committed Christian. In fact, her faith was guiding her decision to be a doctor. There were so many people who needed help.

"You are right, Jennie. Excuse me. I pray now." He bowed his head and was obviously in prayer.

This is awkward, thought Jennie. She turned to leave and there stood Professor Adkins. Again."Excuse me, I'm just leaving," she said as she tried to get past him. Then added, "Did you want to see Samuel?"

"Actually I wanted to see you." Ben Adkins had never spoken a truer sentence. Jennie was becoming an obsession for him. He thought of her on waking and before he fell asleep at night. She had moved to the back of his history class, but he couldn't begin until he had spotted her, made sure she was there. He was using any possible excuse to be around her. He even followed her at a distance when she went to the library or the cafeteria. It was getting so bad that Dr. John and Dr. Gene had warned him he was playing with dynamite, that if he wanted to keep his job he had better knock it off. People were beginning to notice.

Meanwhile Jennie gave him no encouragement, turning away whenever she saw him. Her smiles were all for others. He longed to bask in the happiness of her laughter. He knew his friends were right, but he couldn't help himself. He was hopelessly in love with her, which was stupid to think because he didn't really know her at all.

With a sigh Jennie said, "Well, here I am." Then added coolly, "What is it that you want?" Ben wanted to say "I want you" but instead he stumbled with, "I wanted to know if you needed another chaperone for the trip to Kenya? If you do, I'd be glad to go."

The last thing Jennie wanted was to have this nuisance of a professor along for a whole month. She remembered Sue. "Well, thanks for the offer but we just brought the last chaperone on board. All filled up." She turned to make sure Samuel had heard her. He had finished praying and now nodded assent to her statement. So that was it. Sue Williams would be going to Kenya. Jennie hoped she had made the right decision.

But Ben wasn't through. "Oh, about that paper we discussed? I'm going to submit it into a history competition if that's all right with you."

Jennie didn't think much of the paper she had written. She had done better lots of times, but if he wanted to enter the paper, fine. Maybe it would win a prize and look good on her entrance application to med school.

"Sure. Go ahead. Whatever." And with that she forced Ben to step aside so she could pass. The sweet smell of her hair stayed with him the rest of the day. Sometimes it made him quiver. Just a little.

That night he remembered what Dr. Gene had said to him: "Call her Out-of-Here because that's what you'll be." He sat down at his desk and began to write like a schoolboy, over and over until the paper was full, Out-of-Here, Out-of-Here, Out-of-Here....

## 11.

The more Meghan ignored her parents, Angie and Ron, the more they ignored each other. Her anger at being "stripped of a brother or sister" filled almost every telephone conversation in the few times she called home. It was with fear that Angie moved about the kitchen preparing the food for the next day. It would be a sad Thanksgiving unless she could somehow get through to Meghan that not all decisions in life are perfect, and that her parents weren't perfect.

For that matter it was evident that their marriage was not perfect. Ron was finding many reasons to be away from the house and when he was there he rarely spoke to Angie. When they first found out that Meghan knew Angie had an abortion in college, they tried to discuss their daughter's attitude, but every conversation ended with Ron reminding Angie that she had made the choice, not him. When Angie would say it was a mutual decision, Ron refused to accept any responsibility and would become icily angry, leave the house, and not return for hours. Angie felt like she was living with a stranger. The many years of their marriage seemed nothing to Ron.

Car doors slammed in the driveway and Angie heard raised voices coming toward the house, signaling that Ron had picked up Meghan at the airport per their plan. Immediate arguing, however, wasn't part of the plan.

"Oh God," Angie prayed as she untied her apron, "help us all survive this. Please give us the right words to talk to each other." She turned with open arms to Meghan as the two of them came into the kitchen.

Meghan crossed her arms, refusing her

mother's embrace, saying "I'll take my things upstairs to my room. Call me when dinner's ready." With that she turned on her heels and disappeared.

Ron glared at Angie. "This is quite a mess you got us into," he said through gritted teeth. "I've been bombarded all the way home."

Angie turned toward the sink, picked up her peeler and almost ripped the skins off of the potatoes she had been peeling. She said nothing. What was there to say? They could not undo that long-ago decision. But it had been *their* decision, not hers alone. And why couldn't Ron be more reasonable? Why was he choosing to punish her day after day? What had happened to the love that she thought had existed between them such a short time ago? All those words of how proud he was of her, what a wonderful woman she was, how much she had helped his career? Where had that all gone?

Quietly she asked, "Are we going to the Thanksgiving service tonight?

"Not if your daughter has anything to do with it. She stated flatly on the way home that she didn't want to see any of our friends. Just hers. Too embarrassing to see people who thought we were such great Christians when we're just hypocrites and have been all our married lives. And she hoped we hadn't invited my parents for dinner tomorrow because she couldn't bear to be around them since they probably didn't know about the abortion either. She's on quite a trip!"

Angie loved the Thanksgiving service. It gave her such a feeling of community when the congregation sang, "We gather together to ask the Lord's blessing...." She lifted her head and turned to face Ron. "Well, shall we go then, just the two of us?"

Ron looked steadily at his wife. Guiltily. She

didn't deserve what he was doing to her. He knew
he was hiding his own weakness, his inability to
face up to their daughter's anger. The abortion
wasn't Angie's fault. It was his. He was the one
who had pushed her into sex before they were
married and he had panicked when she became
pregnant. Then, like now, it was about his
reputation, not their commitment to each other. And
the distance between them was his fault, too. He
couldn't face Angie with the truth that he had lost
two major clients and his business was failing.
Getting Meghan through this year tuition-wise was
going to take a small miracle. He had already spent
most of his investments just to keep the business
afloat.

"Ron?" was Angie's soft word.

"What do we have to be thankful for? No! I
won't go! If you want to go, you have car keys.
You can pray for all of us. But it won't do any
good." He turned on his heels and disappeared into
the rest of the house, leaving a forlorn Angie
weeping quietly as she finished peeling the
potatoes. At least she would prepare a wonderful
dinner for tomorrow and perhaps Ron and Meghan
would soften their attitudes when they were full of
such great food.

Thursday morning was cold and windy, even a
hint of snow in the air. When Angie came
downstairs Meghan was already sitting at the
kitchen table, sipping from a mug of hot coffee.

"Good morning, daughter!" Angie said
brightly. "The service was wonderful last night. I
wish you had gone with me."

"I noticed Dad didn't go. At least he knows
better than to go there with all the people you've
known in your life who think you're such a goody
two shoes! How could you be such a….a…. double

person? All sweet and light on the outside but filled with a black sin on the inside? How could you, mother? How could you?"

Meghan got up, turned her back to Angie, and stared out the window. She was silent for a moment, then whirled around, pointing an accusing finger at her mother. "And Dad, making me go through that promise ceremony to wait till I'm married to have sex, and having me wear that stupid promise ring when he didn't wait, you didn't wait! Why did you play me for such a fool? Why didn't you treat me like an adult and tell me what had happened to you? Why did you let me think nothing wrong had ever happened? Why..." Meghan's voice crumbled into tears of hurt and anger.

Angie wanted to take her into her arms and comfort her like she did when she was a little girl, when the tears came after a tumble or a disappointment. But she couldn't move toward Meghan lest she make it worse between them.

"Meghan, what we did was between us, a part of our private marriage, our private world. But we have regretted it ever since and we didn't want you to go through the same thing, or worse. The promise ceremony was our way of trying to keep you out of harm's way. But there was no reason to tell you."

"No reason?" Meghan exploded. "No reason? Letting me grow up alone because you couldn't have another child? And what's that all about? You never told me why you couldn't have another child. What's the story behind that fanciful tale? Scar tissue from the abortion? How did you have me? Or did you? Am I adopted and you haven't told me that either?"

Meghan was leaping from one fanciful idea to

the next, believing her own words as she went. She wasn't even their child; she was sure of it. Or did her mother have artificial insemination? Maybe she had a surrogate mother. All those things were possible in her mind right now.

Angie sank into a chair by the table, covered her face with her hands and began to sob. Such cruel words, and all true. There was too much scar tissue and she couldn't have a child, so they had used insemination and paid a surrogate to carry Meghan to term. But she was not adopted. She was their own flesh and blood.

At that moment Ron stepped into the kitchen. It was over. All the carefully hidden secrets he had heard his daughter say. This time he was the one who spoke quietly, drawing on an inner strength he did not know he had.

"Yes, Meghan. Your mother couldn't have another child because of scar tissue from the abortion. You were not adopted, but we did have to resort to artificial insemination to have you, and you were carried by a surrogate mother." With each word Ron felt he was becoming a stronger person. "You remember that we told you we moved shortly after you were born. We wanted a fresh start, away from anyone who would know about your birth or question why. Your mother and I have paid dearly for that abortion. We both have mourned for that child we didn't have. If we had it to do over again we would have married right then and kept the baby. But we were young. We didn't know how our choice then would adversely affect the rest of our lives."

Meghan was dumbstruck. She had guessed right, even beyond her craziest ideas. But she was not adopted. She was their child. They were her real parents. Yet, "Who was the surrogate? Do I know her? Does she know me?"

This time it was Angie who spoke. "No, you don't know her. Our doctor found her for us, and she wasn't interested in anything but money. She had a family to provide for so she, she ..." Angie paused. How do you say the woman just rented out her womb, but that's what she did. It wasn't the first time she had done it.

Meghan finished her sentence. "She just had me and disappeared, right?"

"You might say that, Meghan. Actually she didn't disappear. She had agreed to a certain amount of money, but she demanded more each month until you were born." Ron remembered how they had scraped together the money, how she had threatened to abort the baby if they didn't pay her more.

"So how much did I cost you?" Meghan demanded. "Huh? How much?"

"In today's money it doesn't sound like much, but nineteen years ago it was quite a lot. Do you really want to know that, Meghan?"

"I suppose not. It wouldn't make any difference, anyway. First you kill a baby and then you tell me I wasn't a product of your love making, isn't that right? And I didn't even come into this world from my own mother. What a piece of work you two are. I don't even know you!"

Meghan paused to catch her breath. It was all too much for her to take in. "Some Thanksgiving this is. Well, you love birds have dinner together but count me out. I've got a friend who lives not far from this town who could only be home for the day. He's my ride back to campus this afternoon. I'm sure not going to stick around here and find out what other horror stories you've got to dump on me." She started to leave the kitchen.

"Wait, Meghan," Ron said as he took her arm and pulled her back. "Please sit down. I'm not finished and there is another horror story, or it could be." Angie looked at her husband with surprise, wondering what they had left out of their confession.

"You need to hear this, both of you. I've been acting badly for almost two months, being angry and cold toward you, Angie, and I'm sorry. Really sorry. I love you. I hope you know that and if you have doubted it, please accept my apology. I'll try to make it up to you. But the fact is that I've lost my best clients and my business is failing. I tried to cover it up. I've used our investments just to keep the doors open and Meghan in college, but unless I get some new clients soon, we could lose the house. I've got a second mortgage on it and the payments are too high. So Meghan, we can make your second semester this year, but then, unless we get a miracle, you'll have to drop out of Callegua in June and go to work. I'm sorry, but at least it's out in the open now." Looking at Angie with pleading eyes he added, "And maybe I can be a decent husband again. I'm so sorry. I wouldn't blame you if you divorced me." His voice trailed off.

No one moved. Silence. A long, awkward pause in the family life of these three decent people who had always loved each other. Later Angie would remember that she felt the whole earth spinning and she was about to be spun off into endless space. Ron had said "divorce", a word never before spoken between them.

Finally Meghan broke the tension by picking up her mug and banging it down on the counter. "I hope you two can work it out. As for me, I'm going back to school while it's still paid for if I can get Joe on the phone. Excuse me." She headed into the family room to make her call, thinking how ironic that she was in a "family" room. Her family had just disappeared.

Minutes later she put her packed weekender bag by the front door and announced that her friend had been called back to campus to fix a computer problem and she would be leaving at eleven. Meghan was relieved to be out of the house before her parents urged her to stay for Thanksgiving dinner.

After Meghan left the kitchen Ron held out his arms to Angie. "Will you forgive me?" he asked. Angie rushed into his embrace. "Of course I forgive you, but what are we going to do?" Her business was growing well but it was not ready to support them all.

Ron answered by placing his lips on hers, then drawing back, smiled and said, "Just what we've always done, until lately. We're going to love each other."

Angie was grateful that their parents had made other plans for the day. After Megan had left, she and Ron took their full Thanksgiving dinner plates outside and sat on the porch steps, side by side in the sun that had emerged at mid-morning. Meghan was gone. Maybe she would never return, this child of their dreams and imaginations. But they would pray for her. When she was ready to love them again, they would be waiting. It was enough for now that they were together again. Whatever their future, they would face it together.

Ron finished his cherry pie. Smiling, he put his arm around Angie's shoulders and gave her a hug. "Great dinner, Angie. Great dinner!" She snuggled against his shoulder. Life was beginning to feel right again. It was truly a wonderful thanksgiving day.

## 12.

On the way back to campus Meghan studied Joe. He seemed like a decent enough guy, a senior, into computers in a big way.

"You look a little down, kid," Joe said. "Tough time at home?"

"Lousy Thanksgiving, that's all. I figured I'd be better off back at an empty campus and I can't wait to get there. Monday seemed a long time away. Thanks for giving me a ride."

Meghan watched the farmland passing by the window. Shuffling through her backpack she found her wallet. There was enough money to eat at the Fry Shack until the cafeteria opened Sunday night. How could her dad let the business fail so she couldn't come back to Callegua? Her insides, no, her brain felt numb, like she had been cast into a foreign land without an interpreter. Foreign land. It was a good thing she hadn't signed up for the Kenya trip. It would have been embarrassing to have to pull out. But she was definitely not going home for interim. Next week she would sign up for a class so she could stay. Her dad would just have to get the money from somewhere to pay for it. So what if they didn't have enough to pay the bills? It served them right. Those two pious people made her sick to her stomach.

Meghan's brain went on and on until it finally wound down into sleep. She woke up as the car swung through Callegua's gates: "Callegua University: Education With A Difference". How many times had she read that and believed it: now she didn't know what to believe. At this moment she wasn't even sure who she was.

"Joe, I've got a little money. Can I help pay for the gas?" she queried.

"No thanks. I was coming anyway. But I'll tell you what you can do. It's been a while for me. How about coming up to my room and having sex?"

So that's the way it is when no one is watching, thought Meghan. Sex was one way to get even with her parents—they did it, and she would too. To Joe she merely shrugged her head and said, "Sure. Sounds like fun. It's been a while for me, too."

Joe was surprised. He had figured her for a virgin and didn't expect her to take him up on his offer. "You sure? I mean, we don't know each other very well."

"What difference does that make?" Meghan responded, an edge in her voice. "As long as you've got condoms. Do you?"

The girl was serious. She sounded experienced and ready. Who was he to turn down an opportunity? "Sure," was Joe's answer.

Meghan tried to put everything she had read into the experience, but she was under whelmed. When she climbed out of Joe's bed an hour later she was disappointed. Sex was no big deal. Not like everybody had made it out to be.

"Where're you going?" asked Joe. "Stay here a little while. Maybe we can have another go."

"Sorry, Joe. I've had a rough day and I need to be alone, so I'm going to my room. Thanks anyway. Some other time maybe." Meghan couldn't believe the casualness in her voice. She had just crossed the big barrier and it meant nothing.

"Well, thanks anyway, Meghan. You sure made my afternoon." Joe was confused. He was sure she was a virgin, but her attitude didn't seem like it. "Oh, by the way, there's a bottle of Vodka on the desk. Somebody gave it to me at home, but I don't like Vodka, so why don't you take it. Have a party with your roommates when they come back." "Sure. Thanks." Meghan picked up the bottle and left the room before Joe could catch on that she had never had a drink in her life, never had sex, never did anything her parents didn't approve of. Those days were over. From now on she'd do whatever she pleased.

Back at her empty room she stripped off her clothes, took a shower to wash off the male smell, pulled on some fresh jeans and a shirt, with the idea of a short nap before hunting for food. The Vodka bottle called to her: try me. Dixie cup in hand she took her first drink of alcohol and waited. Nothing happened except she liked the taste. She was sure something was supposed to happen: she would feel funny or go to sleep or laugh hysterically or sing. Nothing. So she filled the cup again, and this time instead of sipping it, she gulped it down. Fire! There, she'd done it. In one afternoon she had broken the two biggest taboos: sex and alcohol. Not bad. To celebrate her coming out, she'd have a party by herself. Time for her nap, but first another cup of Vodka.

It was dark when she woke up. Where was she? Why did her head bang so? It all came rushing back: her parents, her birth, her father's business failing, sex, Vodka. She stumbled out of bed, used the bathroom, and then started hunting for food in her roommate's desk drawers. Finally she found a candy bar and a granola bar. She quickly consumed them both and washed them down with Vodka. With nothing else to do, she fell back on her bed and into a deep sleep.

On Friday, Meghan managed to get to the Fry Shack, had some breakfast about eleven o'clock, then went exploring campus to see what buildings were open. In the library she found Joe working on one of the computers. She was surprised that she felt nothing special toward him, except unexpectedly she wanted sex. "Hi, Joe.

"Great. Campus is really dead. You're the only action around here."

"Yeah, I guess I am. Want more?" She was shocked at her own question.

"Sure. You mean it?"

"Of course. If you've got it in you." She laughed.

Soon they were making their way together to Joe's room for a repeat performance. This time Meghan stayed a little longer. She was beginning to like this new wild and free person she was turning into.

"Did you try the Vodka?" Joe asked, as she was getting ready to leave.

"I had a couple of sips. It's not too bad. Not as bad as you said."

"Well, take it easy. It's pretty potent stuff." Joe had passed out on less.

"Sure thing. Thanks for the sex. It was good." And Meghan left.

After lunch she walked around the empty campus. She had rebelled against her parents' rules —the ones they never kept—and the numbness was going away. In its place she felt reckless, like she could do anything that would hurt them and it would be all right. The Pro-Life Club would be her biggest thing. And sex. She was sure there were more guys than Joe who would like to bed her down. Alcohol went without saying. Grades? She wasn't that stupid. She'd keep her grade points up so she could transfer somewhere cheaper: she had her future to think of. Maybe she'd bring down a professor, get him involved with her, and then report him. That would cause a stir! Or why bother with a professor, maybe the president. After all, he was married. Yes, he'd be a very good target, and her parents would be totally humiliated. It would take some real ingenuity, but she could do it. Look how easy it had been with Joe.

Saturday, Meghan drew up a list of targets so she could cross each one off when she accomplished it. She had another rendezvous with Joe but told him not to expect such service when classes started. He agreed. Actually, he had a girlfriend, so he was relieved to be out of trouble so easily.

After dinner with her campaign against her parents in order and her roommates arriving the next day, Meghan settled down with a book and the rest of the Vodka. That was the way Jennie found her on Sunday, but the bottle was empty and she was dead drunk.

Meghan's rebellion had begun.

### 13.

Jennie sang happily as she drove back to campus. Her mother had planned a perfect Thanksgiving holiday, inviting all her high school friends that were home to their annual Pie and Polar Bear celebration. Everyone had arrived at 4 p.m. when the sun was getting low and the water in the pool cooling off. This year was special because it was probably the last year they could be together, what with so many moving off the farms and the pace of life busier for everyone.

It had been such fun through the years, starting when she was eight. Her dad had installed the huge above ground pool so she and her friends could swim all summer. Usually after Labor Day he emptied it, put the cover on to keep it clean, and called swimming officially over for the summer.

Then she and her girlfriends had this crazy idea. They had read about Polar Bear swimmers who braved icy waters one day a year, so they decided it would be great fun to take a Polar Bear dip on Thanksgiving Day. While they were at it, they included a pie-eating contest. Everyone brought leftover pie from Thanksgiving dinner and whoever stayed in the pool the longest was awarded a medal that was passed around year after year. Then came the pie eating contest: who could eat the most pie in three minutes was the champion who took home one of her mother's best pies to share with their family. Jennie chuckled as she thought of the times it had snowed, or once when ice formed on the pool, how her dad fussed about leaving the water that late in the year. But the idea took hold and for eleven years it had been the highlight of Thanksgiving. What a gift from her dad that was! She had been devastated when he was killed in the tractor accident, but now it seemed her mother was managing well. That was good for Jennie because it meant there was money for med school. Further, she didn't have to worry about taking care of her mother; she was taking care of herself just fine.

Arriving at campus she parked behind the dorm, grabbed her bag and backpack, and headed to the front where she had to check in. Professor Ben Adkins was sitting on the front steps.

No! Not him again, was Jennie's thought.

"Jennie!" Ben called out. "I've been waiting for you. Good news!" He was waving a thick envelope, which he thrust into her hand when he was close enough.... too close for Jennie's comfort zone.

She stepped back, looking at the return address. It was not familiar. She hadn't a clue where the letter had come from.

"Go ahead. Open it," urged Ben, all the while aware that he was physically reacting to being so close to her and reminding himself "Out-of-Here."

Jennie took several sheets of paper out of the envelope and scanned the first. Her history paper had won a contest of some kind. That would be the one Professor Adkins had asked if he could enter for her. She read on. The prize was a full scholarship to the graduate school of her choice! In a moment she grasped the significance of what she held in her hand: a free ride through med school! But maybe it was limited to history study. She went back to the top of the cover letter and this time read it carefully, slowly.

Ben could scarcely stand the suspense. She was taking so long. Maybe she didn't understand what a great thing this was for someone planning to endure the long years of medical school—and it was anywhere she wanted to go. When he had found the contest on his computer late one night, he was sure this was a way he be with Jennie legitimately. There were papers to fill out, a press release to draw up, and permits from her mother to allow publicity that might include television interviews of Jennie's background, home, education. She was such an outstanding student that he was sure she could win. And joy of joy, she had!

At last Jennie was convinced the contest and prize were genuine. "Oh, Dr. Adkins, thank you! My mother will be as thrilled as I am! Thank you! Thank you!"

Ben wished she had flung her arms around his neck in celebration, but he stayed composed enough to say, "Come by my office sometime this week and we'll get all the papers ready. There's a deadline that has to be met or the prize will move to the runner-up."

"I'll be there tomorrow afternoon, if that's ok," replied Jennie. "Now excuse me. I have to go tell my roommates!" And a joyous Jennie skipped up the steps and disappeared into the dorm.

## 14.

Tomorrow, thought Ben as he walked across campus. He could hardly wait. You did well, Professor Adkins, he told himself. Not only did he have a reason to be close to Jennie, but also, he had paid the way for this girl of his dreams to fulfill her dream of becoming a doctor. His joy was evident when he met his friends, John and Gene, who were so full of their own news that they didn't give Ben a second glance. They wanted to know where he stood on letting the president go.

"You know," said John, "you'll probably have to choose which side you are on at the next faculty meeting."

"Are you serious?" Ben asked. "Over a movie? Who's heading this up, anyway?" He thought the move to oust President Clayton was coming from the ultra-conservative religion department, but he could be wrong.

It was Dr. Gene who answered. "Ever since Clayton was chosen, the faculty members who wanted another candidate have been unhappy. They've just been waiting for a chance to muscle Clayton out and put their man in—a guy from Texas, I think. So when Clayton was spotted coming out of this X-rated film, they knew they could get him for not setting the right example for the students. It's some people from almost every department, except the Arts, of course. They're pretty steamed for a different reason. So far as they're concerned it is the quality of the film that is important, no matter what it's rating. But nobody listens to the Arts, you know, low on the totem pole and all that."

Dr. John chimed in, "As far as I can tell, Clayton's doing a good job. He raised over five million dollars last year without a major campaign. No president we have had has done that in a long time.

Dr. Gene finished with, "He'd better keep his nose clean with nary a slip-up or he's history!"

Ben was amazed at the nonchalance his friends exhibited over such an important action. Clayton was the only president he had known, and he seemed like a decent Christian person, well spoken, and with the college in his heart. And his background was terrific: Ph.D. from Harvard, M.S. and B.S. from Yale, and three years of Bible college before that. He had been both faculty and administration, then academic dean at a major school before applying at Callegua. What more could they want?

The three friends turned to discussing their Thanksgiving break, came to a fork in the sidewalks, said their "see ya's", with Gene and John heading to the library and Ben to his office. As an afterthought Gene turned around and called out to Ben: "Oh, Ben, how's it going with Out-Of-Here? Take a lesson from what's happening to Clayton!"

Ben shivered in his soul at Gene's warning. He wanted to be successful at Callegua and it looked like Jennie would be the price he had to pay.

## 15.

Jennie had gone up the stairs two at a time to her room, but her roommate hadn't returned. She had to tell someone about winning the contest. Maybe Meghan was back. When there was no answer to her knock on Meghan's door, she tried the

knob and realized the door was unlocked, so maybe
Meghan was in the bathroom and didn't hear her.
She pushed the door open and was hit by the sour
smell of vomit. The room was a mess; the
wastebasket was spilled and its contents covered
with vomit. There was a trail into the bathroom.
Meghan must be sick, was Jennie's first thought.

Forgetting her news, she stepped carefully
into the room. "Meghan, are you here?" she called.
A moan came from the bottom bunk and Jenny was
immediately at Meghan's side. She reeked of
alcohol and vomit and soiled underclothes. Her
eyes were closed. "Meghan, are you all right?
Wake up. You've messed yourself and we need to
get you cleaned up. Meghan, can you hear me?"

Meghan gave a slight nod. She could hear,
but she was confused. Why was she in her room?
Didn't she go home for Thanksgiving vacation?
Her head was pounding, and her clothes felt like she
had wet the bed. That couldn't be; only little
children did that. She tried to look at Jennie but her
eyes just wouldn't focus and when she spoke her
words made no sense; she couldn't get the words
out.

Jennie was bewildered. She knew Meghan
didn't drink, but even with Jennie's limited
experience with alcohol, she was pretty sure
Meghan was drunk, and that she had made herself
sick was evident by the vomit everywhere in the
room. Getting a cold wet washcloth from the
bathroom, Jennie washed Meghan's face, then
wiped off her hands. She didn't know what else to
do. Except clean up. It took her almost a half hour
to put the room back in order, wipe up the vomit,
and clean the bathroom that appeared to have taken
a major hit. Meghan kept struggling to focus mind.

"Jennie," she finally spoke clearly. "My
parents are liars…they killed a baby… My mother

didn't even carry me, had a surr...surro...surrogate do it...they never told me... I hate them...they're such hypocrites...I don't think they're even Christians...I really hate them..." and with that she turned her head toward the wall and passed out again.

Jennie realized that Meghan was beyond hearing. Obviously she had suffered something traumatic when she was at home, but this wasn't the time to try to talk about it. Quietly she left the room, closing the door behind her. At least when Meghan's roommates came, the room would be in order. That was the best she could do for her friend right now.

She didn't feel like celebrating any more, not after seeing Meghan in such a condition, so she went to her room, took one more look at the award letter, and carefully put it away. Then she went out to the work waiting at her Kenya office space.

It was dark when Meghan finally woke from her drunken stupor. Her roommate was already in bed and the dorm was quiet. She stared into the dark, thinking about what she had just done to her life. She had made a huge break with her parents, perhaps irreparable. Her virginity had been tossed away on a guy she barely knew, but somehow she didn't care. One thing was certain; she never wanted to drink again if it made her so sick. The smell of her clothes soaked in vomit made her nauseas. And underneath all of her thoughts was a huge question: who was she now?

Quietly she slipped out of bed, got a clean nightshirt out of her dresser drawer, and stepped into the bathroom. Emerging from the shower a few minutes later, she studied herself in the full-length mirror on the door. She looked the same except for puffiness around her eyes, but that would go away. It was her eyes that were different. What she saw in them was despair, anger, even hatred. The joy that she had just before Thanksgiving had disappeared. Would anyone else notice that?

Meghan shook off her reverie. She was imagining things. Her stomach growled, but she knew everything on campus was closed. She would just have to tough it out until breakfast.

Tiptoeing back into the room so as not to wake her roommate, Meghan fumbled around on her dresser top until she found her alarm clock, turned the alarm on, and by the nightlight saw it was 1:30 a.m. Why hadn't she bought a lighted clock instead of using the one her father got at a garage sale? The way her dad talked about his business she'd better get used to garage sales.

Suddenly she felt depressed at the thought of leaving Callegua, leaving her friends, especially Jennie, her best friend. How would she tell Jennie? She hated her father for being so stupid as to lose his business! Her hand brushed against something as she moved it away from the alarm clock. It rolled, fell over the edge, and onto the floor. The promise ring. "Well, I'll never need that again," Meghan thought. The sound of it bouncing off into some hidden corner triggered a new emotion inside her: she wanted sex. Nobody told her it was addictive. This was a whole new problem. And as she tossed and turned trying to get comfortable in her bed, her body kept calling out for satisfaction. It was almost three o'clock before she finally dropped into a troubled sleep.

## 16.

David Belkin was pretty sure he wanted to be a minister. At seventeen he had made his commitment to be a Christian and shortly afterward he thought God was telling him to be a minister. It wasn't anything he ever wanted to do; actually he was majoring in engineering. The logical thinking it required was what he liked. Since he was a little kid he had taken things apart to see how they worked, then challenged himself to put them back together again, sometimes better than before. His goal always was to find better ways to make things. In high school he took first prizes at science fairs; sometimes his projects caught the interest of manufacturers, but none had made him any offers. Callegua was his choice because their engineering department was the best in any Christian college. Besides, at Callegua he might find a wife who was bright, educated, and Christian, a perfect combination in his mind. Now that he was a senior, he had started looking....

Jennie had caught his attention early in the semester. Her organization of the Kenya trip was impressive, she was a straight A student, and it didn't hurt that she was also one of the prettiest girls on campus but she didn't seem to know it. David liked that. When he had dropped into a chair beside her in the cafeteria to talk about the trip, she seemed unaware of herself, not bothered by insecurities. Certainly, if he did decide to be a minister he would want a wife who could stay sane in the midst of insane demands. The Kenya trip would prove a real opportunity to get to know Jennie better, as well as to test out his "calling". Seminary would mean three or four more years of graduate school; he could start in engineering with a master's degree. That was a big difference in time and money, plus the engineering department chair had promised to help him with scholarships for his M.S.

"Tough decision," he mused as he crossed campus on his way to chapel. "I've got to keep my mind and spirit open." The twice-weekly chapel was a requirement for all students, with attendance monitored and demerits issued beginning with three absences. David knew graduation could be held up for too many demerits, but chapel was not a bother for him as it was for some students. He spotted Jennie's attractive friend Meghan in the crowd moving into the auditorium. Maybe he should get to know her, too.

Samuel Katata was the speaker this morning, always a popular choice with his many stories from Africa. His heavy accent required careful listening, but it was worth it. From the time Samuel said "Good morning" he had David's full attention, his mind grabbing at the scripture Samuel was reading: "Then Jesus came to them and said, All power in heaven and on earth is given to me. So go and make followers of all people in the world. Baptize them in the name of the Father and the Son and the Holy Spirit. Teach them to obey everything that I have told you. You can be sure that I will be with you always. I will continue with you until the end of the world." (Matthew 28:18-20)

David felt electrified, as if he had been nailed to his seat. He had read those words from Matthew many times before, but this time they were spoken directly to him. Usually calm, David wanted to shout that God had just called him, told him this was what *he* was to do. To document the moment he scribbled the date and time on his notebook and checking in the Bible in the bookrack in front of him, he found the passage and recorded it word for word. He knew! There was no doubt! He was headed for the ministry. Later David could not remember anything Samuel had said, only the powerful moment when scripture spoke to him. He would remember it all his life.

Meghan had noticed David looking at her when she came into the chapel. He looked like a good recruit for her Pro-Life Club. And maybe more, she thought, as the new sensations in her body reminded her. At this point Meghan felt like there was not much point in going on with the club since she wasn't going to stay at Callegua. For that matter, there wasn't much point in studying. Flunking out would give her an excuse not to have to admit why she was really leaving, that her family was broke and she felt totally humiliated. She had stayed away from Jennie for two days: she couldn't face her. And today Jennie was sitting on the platform because she was chairing the Kenya trip, so avoiding her would be pretty easy.

Jennie looked out across the auditorium, spotted Meghan, promised herself to have lunch with her, then stepped to the podium to ask all the students going to Kenya to stand.

"Callegua students, these are your January missionaries. Let's give them a little applause!" After the applause had stopped she added, "And let's hold each person in our prayers and the orphanage in Kenya, that Callegua's students will truly serve God in the month they will be there."

David, still in shock from his scriptural encounter, nevertheless took note of Jennie's poise and words. He was going to be a minister and she looked like just the right kind of helper in such a life. On his notepad he wrote "Jennie Reyes", circled her name, then underlined it for emphasis. "Jennie Belkin" had a nice ring to it.

Across the auditorium another person was scribbling Jennie's name on an index card, only on his card it read "Jennie Adkins", and Ben quickly slipped the card into his pocket lest anyone around him saw it. If only he knew how to claim her, he was sure she would become his wife. A professor and a medical doctor seemed like a perfect combination to him, even if it meant waiting a long time. There would never be anyone else for him.

## 17.

Before Christmas break Doug Williams had sent all the tickets and visas to Jennie. She made sure everyone had their required shots along with a brief physical from the health center. Samuel had double-checked on his student status so there wouldn't be a problem for him to return to finish his senior year after the trip to Kenya. All was in order and eighteen excited students went home to relax before their adventure.

Sue Williams was not quite so excited. In fact, she was dragging her feet all the way. Doug had come home for Christmas just to make sure she didn't back out. "Mom, you'll do great, you'll see. Besides, Trisha is expecting you."

"Trisha? Yeah, I just bet she's expecting me. Dreading is more like it. We didn't get along too well at Callegua. She was on this big Jesus trip and tried to push it down everybody's throats. Nobody was good enough for her. Frankly, Doug, I don't know why I agreed to go. It's going to be a disaster; I just know it!"

"But Mom, it's been over twenty years. It's not the 70's; it's the 90's. She's changed. You've changed. You've got nothing to worry about." Doug was usually very convincing, but Sue was not convinced. Their conversations continued off and on the whole week that Doug was at home.

J.W. was looking forward to Sue's month away. He had some important business deals coming up and he didn't want her interference. He had been able to keep her at bay most of the time by giving her errands to do, or sending her out with a handful of money to shop. It was worth it for the privacy he needed.

Just before Doug left, J.W. approached him with a proposition. "Doug, I've got a business contact in Africa that I want you to make for me. Not a big effort, in fact you could meet him at the airport before you come home. He has some important papers—an agreement between our companies—that we don't want to trust to the mail, so do you suppose you could meet him and bring them home for me? It would really be a big help."

"Sure, Dad," was Doug's reply. He had never been quite sure what his father's business was; he just knew he had business all over the world and it was apparently very profitable. The family had never wanted for money.

"We'll be leaving January 28th. Have to give the students time to get back to campus and catch some zzzz's before they start classes again. So when I get back to the office, I'll email you with the exact times." Then Doug added, "Wait, Mom's ticket is here. I can give you the information now so you can plan ahead. Of course there could be changes, but this should be pretty accurate information." He was glad his dad's request had resulted in his reaching for his mother's ticket from his briefcase, because he had forgotten to give it to her. "Here's Mom's ticket. You can help me, too, and make sure she gets on the plane!"

J.W. smiled as he took the ticket package. "Not to worry, son. She'll be on the plane. And thanks. I really appreciate your help."

Doug slid behind the wheel of his Porsche. "Tell her goodbye for me. I couldn't find her anywhere."

"Sure thing," responded J.W. He watched the car until it was out of sight. With Doug's help he just might pull this deal off. He chuckled with satisfaction, then went in the house to give Sue her ticket. Don't worry, Doug, he thought, your mother will be on that plane. Things were coming together very nicely.

## 18.

Drs. John and Gene slid into the back row of seats beside Ben just as the faculty meeting was about to start.

"This ought to be a hot one. Watch them divide into yeas and nays before the hour is over." Dr. John liked sitting at the top of the lecture hall so he could see everyone, watch their reactions and their whispered conversations to one another. He had been at Callegua so long that he knew everyone on the faculty pretty well. Grinning, he pulled out his yellow tablet and drew up a yea and nay list. He showed it to Ben, adding, "We'll see how close I come." Gene and Ben both gave him a thumbs up sign as the faculty chairman pounded his gavel on the desk. The room was quiet immediately.

"Dr. Adkins, would you please come forward and open our meeting with prayer?" Ben pulled in his breath. He had not been asked to pray aloud in the year and a half he had been at Callegua, and certainly never asked to pray at a faculty meeting. His heart began to race as he stood to comply, moving like an automaton down the lecture hall steps. What would he say? This wasn't fair; he should have been warned. Usually it was a religion professor they called on to do the opening prayer at faculty meetings. Why him?

By the time he reached the front he could think of only two words: "Dear Jesus." His mind was blank, but his soul was crying out for help from God himself. "Dear, dear Jesus," he continued, "We all stand in need of help today." He knew he did, and right now! He paused trying to think of what should come next. The room was very quiet and it gave him an idea: "Let us all take a few moments to consider this meeting in quiet personal prayer." Brilliant, he thought. He waited almost too long before saying; "We thank you for being present in this room, in our personal prayers. Please be with us as we consider the matters at hand. In Jesus name we pray, Amen."

Ben scarcely heard the chairman complement him on his wise prayer when such a difficult decision lay before the faculty that day. All he could think was to get back to his seat as quickly as possible and disappear from everyone's view. John and Gene welcomed him back, both with broad smiles recognizing his discomfort. Gene added, "Good for you. That's over for the rest of the year. They only call on you once."

"Now you tell me," was Ben's response. He guessed he had been spared the first year because he was new, but one thing was sure: if they called on him again, he would have a prayer ready in his pocket.

"Ladies and gentlemen." The chairman began. "I believe we all know that the effectiveness of President Clayton has been challenged. Likewise, we now face the challenge of making our recommendation to the Board of Trustees. Of course, we know it is not binding upon their decision, but we also know that they want to keep us all happy -- if they can." A titter spread across the lecture hall. Keeping everyone on the faculty happy was an impossible task. Someone was always out of sorts over some little thing. It was a running joke among the faculty.

"Therefore I will suggest that we do this as easily as possible. The question is: Shall we ask the President to resign? Let's take a few minutes for each department to canvas its members and then we will take a roll call before we open the meeting up to individual comments. Please begin now and come back to your seats when I sound the gavel." The chairman had thought a long time about this meeting. He wanted to avoid faculty divisions if possible.

Ben, John, and Gene spotted the two other history professors about five rows down from them, and since they were in a relatively quiet spot, motioned the two to join them. Fortunately they had already discussed this issue in their department meeting earlier in the day and were in accord: they thought the whole issue of firing the president over attending an X-rated movie was ridiculous. Clayton was doing a good job and if he were let go over this, maybe they would be next for some scurrilous act. The five agreed that the president should stay. To show their unity they remained seated together.

Ben watched with fascination as some departments were having vigorous debates. One professor walked away from his group, obviously angry. They called him back, but he waved them off and sat down with his arms folded tightly across his chest. The chair of the art department was doing her best to get her group to come to a consensus, but everyone seemed to be talking at once, with much waving of arms and head shaking. The noise level was growing rapidly. Occasionally someone would laugh, lifting the tension a little.

As he watched, Ben wondered what his fate would be if anyone suspected how enamored he was with Jennie. He was still under the radar, at least as far as he knew. Every approach he made was over an academic issue. Nothing romantic had happened and he intended to keep it that way, at least until summer vacation. Maybe then he could visit her off campus....

The gavel brought him sharply back to reality.

The department roll call had begun and Dr. John was marking each vote on his yellow pad. Ben glanced over and saw trouble. The ayes and the nays were evenly divided.

The chairman had also been keeping tabs and watched in dismay as his careful plan failed. It was going to be a long, contentious meeting, just what he wanted to avoid. As the room grew quiet he announced that there was no decision; therefore the floor was open for discussion.

"Mr. chairman, members of the faculty." An engineering professor rose to speak. Ben groaned inside. This man was everything he disliked about the ultra conservatives on the faculty. In his pompous voice he continued. "All of you know the importance of example for teenagers. No one must adhere to example more than the president of this institution. Callegua has a long history of taking care of its students, its faculty showing the utmost respect for the principles of Christianity in our unspoken code. X-rated films are not the place we want our students. They will get ideas for life that might destroy them or at least weaken their faith. But how can we expect students to avoid what our president accepts for himself? This is most egregious behavior, which I personally do not approve, nor do my engineering fellows. The Engineering Department recommends dismissal!" His voice had risen as he spoke, until at the end he was fairly shouting. Other voices shouted their approval. A few stood to applaud. Ben noticed how satisfied the speaker looked as he took his seat.

Hands shot up across the room, everyone wanting to be recognized at once. Voices called out for attention. The chair brought down the gavel: "Gentlemen! Ladies! Let's do this in an orderly fashion, please. We have heard one aye. Who wishes to present a nay?" He was careful not to say, "Who wishes to present a rebuttal." Those would be fighting words.

Several faculty members raised their hands to speak in support of keeping President Clayton and the chair recognized a woman whom Ben knew as an internationally known sociologist. It was her superb publications that had helped him decide to come to Callegua. She stepped to the front of the group, giving her the option of looking everyone in the eye, one by one, as she spoke.

"Gentlemen. Ladies. Esteemed chairman and faculty members: We are not here to discuss our personal taboos, no matter how they are tied to our religious convictions. Our task is to consider the effectiveness of President Clayton as he leads Callegua University. He has been here scarcely enough time for anyone to accomplish much, but has already set a record in fund raising, providing for courses we dearly need and scholarships for some of our most gifted, but poor, students. The X-rated movie is only important if we make it so. Surely you are not so naïve as to think that Callegua students have never been to such a movie, probably with their parents while they were still in high school? It is a non-issue for them, as it should be for us. The president is a Christian with the highest standards in his personal life. His family is a testimony to his witness at home. We in the Sociology Department support him in every way." A cry of "Yes!" and "Hear, hear!" went across the hall.

Back and forth the discussion went. Ben noted that some of the oldest faculty members maintained the most restrictive view of the situation. Those most supportive had been at Callegua five years or less. It was soon obvious that their opinions were not weighed as heavily as the more senior members.

Finally the chairman called for an individual vote and the yeas carried the day. The Trustees would be told that the faculty did not support President Clayton, was in fact calling for his resignation. Further they were supporting one of their own to take his place while a presidential search was conducted. Ben let out a soft groan when he realized that Dr. Ingram, the professor who had spoken for the Engineering Department, was the faculty choice. Ben believed this choice did not auger well for the college.

The word had already spread among the students by dinnertime, even before President Clayton was told. By the next morning several of the best students had determined to transfer to a college that had a more rational view of the world of the 90's.

Meghan saw this as a perfect excuse to use for not returning next year.

Jennie decided to discuss this with her mother at Christmas break. She couldn't risk a lowered college evaluation when she applied to med school.

Ben made an appointment with the dean of a nearby state university to discuss hiring into their faculty.

David was glad he was graduating in June. He had already put his application in to seminary, so Callegua could do whatever they wanted. His future was set.

Dr. John and Dr. Gene shrugged their shoulders and sat on the committee to choose a new president, deciding the safest thing to do was to just go with the flow. No doubt this would happen many times before they reached retirement. Besides, Gene would have tenure at the end of the next school year, and he didn't want to mess that up. Life at Callegua wasn't all that bad.

Only Samuel Katata got down on his knees and prayed for President Clayton and his family.

## 19.

Christmas vacation dragged for some students, like Meghan, who in spite of her efforts had nowhere else to go but home during the school break. She stayed in her room or sullenly responded when either of her parents spoke to her. She got food from the kitchen when no one was there, and on Christmas morning ignored the tree and gifts designed for her. When Angie pressed her to take the gifts, she left the room with a "Never! Not from two hypocrites!" Both Ron and Angie were glad when the vacation ended and Meghan left for school. Afraid of pushing her farther away from them, they had somehow managed to scrape together the money for the interim class she insisted on taking.

At Jennie's house the vacation whizzed by. She and her mother, Joan, were in town several days in a row trying to get everything that was on her list for Kenya. Beside her own things, which meant digging out her summer clothes for the tropical climate, everyone was to bring gifts for the children at the orphanage to suit the child assigned to them. In November, true to her promise, Trisha had sent pictures of each child. At the team meeting the photos were all put into a paper bag, which was passed around for each person to draw two pictures. Jennie had drawn a brother and sister, Daniel and Priscilla, which were their Biblical names. Priscilla was just three; Daniel, seven, but both were so under nourished that it was difficult to see what age they were.

Jennie had taken the pictures back to her room after the meeting, mounted them on cardboard, and pinned them on the bulletin board above her desk. Each morning as she gathered her books to go to classes, she prayed for them. When she sat to study in the late afternoon, she prayed for them. And the last thing before she slept was her prayer for Daniel and Priscilla. She didn't know exactly what to pray but that didn't make any difference. God could figure out what they needed. All she knew was that their parents had died of AIDS, and after their grandmother died, they had come to live at the orphanage. Jennie already loved them.

Shopping was great fun. Joan entered into Jennie's excitement and together they began to stuff the duffle bag Jennie was allowed to take.

"Oh, look, mother!" Jennie was holding up a dark-skinned doll she found at the back of a display. "Priscilla has to have this!" Minutes later they discovered an inflatable ball. It would pack flat. Daniel would surely like that. Suitable clothes were hard to find since only winter things were on display, so Jennie went on the Internet to outfit the children. Her own things fit in a small carry-on bag, but the duffle bag was bulging by the time she was ready to leave. She would go first to Callegua and then travel on the campus bus to the airport in Chicago, Chicago to London, a couple of hour's layover, and on to Nairobi's Jomo Kenyatta airport. It would take them twenty hours if there was no delay.

"Jennie, I am so proud of you!" Joan was proud of herself as well. She had done a good job raising this girl, this young woman. "I'm a little afraid for you, too. Please don't take risks. You know there are guerrilla fighters in Kenya and they hate the Christians. Don't put yourself in harm's way if you can help it." Joan paused. "I agreed to this because I knew Trisha well. I knew that she would not have the group come if it was dangerous, but we may know more about what's happening in Kenya than she does. So please, please be careful."

Joan straightened her shoulders, then added, "But enough of warnings. Have a great time! Come back full of stories to tell me. And take lots of pictures. You've got your digital camera, haven't you?" It had been her Christmas gift to Jennie.

"Don't worry so, mom. I'll be just fine. And yes, my camera is right here in the outside pocket of my bag so I can grab it quickly if I see a picture that just has to be taken. And now I'm off. Give me a kiss!"

Anyone watching would have seen the love flow between them: the daughter off on a great adventure, the mother waiting anxiously at home. Such is the fate of the generations.

As Jennie left, Joan watched her without envy, content with her farm business and home. But her heart skipped a beat when she thought about all that might confront her young daughter. She paused as she walked back to the house, looked up at the graying sky, and said aloud, "OK, God. You take over. She's all yours, anyway."

Jennie was well aware of the danger that might confront the team. She had discussed it with Samuel and President Clayton when the invitation first came from Trisha. Frequently she had quizzed Doug Williams as he made the travel arrangements for the group: what were the travel warnings? Had the U.S. government made any statements? How active were the rebels? His responses had always been soothing, calming her fears and encouraging her with the great value this would be to the students who went. And Trisha's emails were so full of excitement and anticipation. All of these emails were shared with the eighteen students and the chaperones from campus, but Sue received only those items that Doug decided to send her, which were confined to travel and visa arrangements.

Sue had prepared, however. Reluctantly she had gotten her inoculations, hunted and found her passport, had it updated, and filled her suitcase with lovely summer clothes. Just because she was going on a "work" team, she didn't need to look run down or tacky. However, in a trunk in the attic she had found the Callegua football windbreaker J.W. had given her during that disastrous freshman year and decided it might help the students to relate to her, so it was stuffed in with one pair of shabby jeans. She would definitely be "shabby chic" on this trip.

Then there was the problem with her hair. Sue was used to having her hairdresser come to the house whenever something important was coming up, so she never really tended to her hair by herself. The compromise was to cut it very short, but stylish, so she only needed to wash it and let it dry. She understood electricity was in short supply at the orphanage, so even a hair dryer was out of the question. With her hairdresser's advice, she settled on a modified spiked style, which she deemed a success when J.W.'s eyebrows went up and he became amorous. To herself she thought that she should have done this long ago. Maybe he would have stayed more interested in her.

Sue was to meet the group at Chicago's O'Hare International Airport. Armed with the flight schedule and terminal number, she stepped into the airport shuttle that Doug had arranged. Finally a tinge of excitement was beginning to take hold so that she had to admit this could be a real adventure in her otherwise placid life. She still felt uneasy about meeting Trisha again, but it would be fun to mix with college students, maybe discuss real ideas again, and even do something to help the children.

J.W. certainly wasn't sorry to see her leave; he almost seemed happy to be alone. Sometimes he was a complete mystery to her.

The trip to the airport was shorter than she had anticipated. Doug was waiting for the shuttle and quickly gathered her bags and led her to the student group.

"Hey, gang, this is my mom. She's the other chaperone going with us, so you better stay sharp around her!" was his introduction of Sue. Quickly she added, "And my name is Sue, not Mom!" to the amusement of the students.

A whirl of names followed as they called out to her, and she was swept up in the confused excitement until she heard the name "Jennie". So this was Joan's girl: A beautiful young woman, obviously in charge and competent, so different from the college student Sue had roomed with more than twenty years before.

## 20.

Jennie watched Sue from the edge of the group. Sue was the girl who had dragged her mother into drugs and alcohol, and almost got her raped during that freshman year. The story was fresh in Jennie's mind because she had reviewed it often when she found out that Sue was coming with the group. Samuel was also studying this new person, this "chaperone" with the beautiful clothes and stylish hair. Hopefully she had brought work clothes, otherwise she wouldn't fit in at all. Perhaps it had been a mistake to let her come, but Doug had been so insistent that there was little option.

This wasn't the time for either Jennie or Samuel to size up the situation. They had to make sure everyone's luggage was checked, and each passport had visa stamps and was available, not packed away in checked baggage, which the group had been warned about. David Belkin had come back to campus with a cold, so everyone else had been asked to keep their distance from him so the virus wouldn't spread through the whole group. Before leaving campus, Jennie and Samuel had gone over a packing checklist with everyone at their final campus meeting. As group leaders they were carrying extra medical supplies: "starters and stoppers", general antibiotics from the health center, and first aid items. In addition, they had both been praying for a safe and healthy trip.

Jennie was impressed with Doug Williams. He was bright, energetic, organized, completely and confidently in charge. She had to admit that he was also very good looking. Her head gave her heart a warning: med school.

Doug, on the other hand, was immediately attracted to Jennie. She was the raven-haired beauty he had imagined, and really smart! Nothing had been left to chance in her planning for this trip, and the group showed it: they were excited but at ease, a mark of their confidence in Jennie and Samuel's work. The two faculty members accompanying the group were almost unnecessary. Doug decided this was definitely going to be an interesting trip, what with his mother's new experiences and Jennie.

His mother was a problem, however, thought Doug. The way she was dressed was so out of step with where they were going and what they were going to do in Kenya. Like Samuel, he hoped that in that heavy suitcase Sue had brought there were some old work clothes. He chuckled to himself at that thought: she didn't own any old work clothes. Everything in her closet was a designer copy. Doug doubted she even owned a pair of jeans. Well, she was still slender; maybe she could borrow some from the students....

When Doug, Jennie, and Samuel were content that everyone had arrived with passports in order, they moved through the gates as a group, each having checked one bag and carrying a smaller one with a full change of clothes in case the luggage was lost or did not arrive in Kenya with them. The group's excitement increased as they moved into the gate waiting area. Jennie could almost tell which ones might be trouble and which would cling to her or Samuel. Alice Dakin would bear watching; she was already flirting with Chris Conrad. No doubt there would be more than one romance before the month was over.

This was an adventure in leadership for Jennie. She was glad Doug was there as her resource in travel, and Samuel as her helper in Kenya. While Jennie surveyed the group, Sue flitted around from student to student, introducing herself and gleaning a bit of the personality of each young person. Doug watched his mother with surprise. Her behavior was totally unlike the society matron she was at home. She seemed full of energy, curious about the students, interested in all that was happening. It had been years since she had shown interest in anything but shopping. Well and good, he mused to himself. Maybe this trip would give her life a new course.

When the flight number was called, the students again moved as a group. Doug's careful work paid off as their seats were all together, which pleased everyone. Sue found herself next to her son. She would rather have been with a student, but she told herself this was an opportunity to get reacquainted after these years of separation. She knew almost nothing about his personal life, whether he had ever had a serious girlfriend, what kind of place he lived in, what he did for amusement. He was almost a stranger. With that thought she settled into her seat with anticipation of the long flight ahead.

Doug, squatting in the bulkhead space in front of Jennie and Samuel, found his opportunity to get acquainted with Jennie by going over the flight routes and requirements for entering Kenya, with Samuel listening closely. Much had changed since he left his homeland three and a half years before and Samuel wanted to have current knowledge to fulfill his responsibilities as Kenya leader. His concentration was difficult, for his mind was filled with images of his wife and children walking the roads to reach the mission. Even more dominant were his thoughts on their reunion: he was impatient to arrive. Samuel quickly realized that Doug was concentrating on giving the information just to Jennie and also rightly surmised that Doug was more interested in Jennie than in the information he was giving.

To the group and especially to Sue, the flight was interminable, even with Doug beside her. He only talked about the trip, not about himself or his work or his personal life. He was as distant now as when he had left home after finishing his two-year college degree. From the clothes he wore at Christmas, the Porsche he was driving and his gifts to her and J.W., Sue decided he was making good money. But here on the plane he quickly fell asleep and Sue was left to the magazine she found in the seat pocket.

Although there was satisfaction in the constant droning of the engines, the hours seemed twice as long as at home. When the pilot at last announced that they would soon be landing in London, everyone in the group quickly roused from their half-sleep, and began talking excitedly. Sue was amazed how smooth the flight had been: only one spot of turbulence in the whole trip. But it was a tired bunch of college kids that walked off the plane in London. Doug and Samuel had helped everyone get their bags from the overhead compartments, and Doug had waited with Jennie to make sure all were safely off and accounted for. David Belkin got off last, bleary eyed and red nosed. He turned his head so Jennie wouldn't see how terrible he looked: no way to start a courtship!

The layover was long enough to allow the students to peruse the airport stores and fast food places while they waited, although this gave Jennie great concern lest someone did not arrive back in time for the plane to Nairobi. Her concern was unnecessary, however, for no one strayed very far. Like Jenny, they were afraid of missing the flight. So when the loading call came, each one was waiting with passport in hand. Doug counted them, Jennie identified each one, and Samuel stood at the gate entrance to verify that each had actually boarded.

The three were relieved as they settled into their seats for this last leg of the journey. As soon as lunch had been served the plane grew very quiet; almost all the passengers were asleep. Only Sue sat wide-eyed, wondering what lay ahead, how Trisha would receive her, realizing how inappropriate were the clothes she had brought, and curious about Doug's obvious attraction to Jennie. The irony of Joanie's daughter and her son together was not lost on Sue. But at last even she was consumed by weariness and fell fast asleep.

Sometime during the flight, dinner was served and the passengers began to rouse, getting up in the aisles, using the restrooms. The buzz between the students began again as their excitement grew. The pilot announced the temperature in Nairobi, the capitol of Kenya where they would be landing. The mission was to have transportation at the airport to take them the rest of the way. Samuel was fully awake now, and no one could have measured his anticipation as he drew near to his homeland and family. He knew he had to return to Callegua for his final semester, but it would be so much easier after seeing that his Zaporra, Lydia, and Paul were safe and in good health,

Jennie was weighing the responsibility she had taken on for the college. It was during the layover in London that it hit her: If something happened to one of the students, she was the first person in charge. Had she taken on too much? Samuel and Doug would help, of course, but Samuel was not a U.S. citizen, and Doug was not affiliated with Callegua. She wasn't sure what the two college-assigned faculty members would do since they had taken only minimal interest in the trip. Accordingly, while they were on layover, she had reviewed with Doug the insurance each one carried and the options in case of sickness or accident.

Now, on impulse, she changed seats with the student next to Sue. This was as good a time as any to find out how much help this "chaperone" would be in an emergency.

"Jennie, darling, I'm so looking forward to getting to know you. Your mother and I were roommates at Callegua, you know. Isn't it amazing that we are here together and going to the mission that another of our roommates established! Doug just insisted that I come, you know. I do hope the students will accept me." As the words gushed from Sue, she reached over and patted Jennie's knee. Not waiting for a response she went on: "And here you are, all grown up, beautiful, in charge. I can scarcely believe that you are Joanie's daughter!" Then realizing how her words must sound to Jennie, Sue added, "Your mother was quite shy in college, you know. But we all loved her."

Jennie felt a shock go through her at this enormous lie, but she composed herself, responding with "My mother is very competent now. She runs a commercial farm by herself, overseeing many employees, and is a very successful business woman."

"But isn't she married? I heard that she married Jim. That was a real surprise after what they went through in her freshman year."

"When she was a senior, Jim came to campus searching for her. They had both matured by then, and they discovered a deep love for each other. Unfortunately my father passed away when I was in high school."

"I'm so sorry," Sue said with another pat on Jennie's knee. "I didn't know. We sort of lost touch over the years."

Jennie decided that was all of her background she wanted to share with this woman, so she launched into her purpose for sitting next to Sue. "Tell me, Sue. How do you see yourself fitting into the role of chaperone for this group? I understand you knew Trisha when you were at Callegua. What are you expecting to find?"

Sue flushed, wondering how much Jennie knew about that freshman year, Trisha on her Jesus trip, beautiful Angie who was such a leader, and Joanie whom she had led deeper and deeper into drugs until the night Joan had bolted away from her gang of guys and left her at their mercy. After they were married J.W. had filled her in on all the details of that night: thinking about it still horrified her. She looked carefully at Jennie, so composed, waiting for her answer. Jennie doesn't know, Sue decided before answering.

"Jennie, you're in charge. You know everyone and what's supposed to happen. If it's all right with you I will stay in the background and fill in wherever you need me. I've already met some of the group: they're wonderful kids."

"First, they don't think of themselves as kids, Sue," was Jennie's reply. "All but a few are adults by law, so we will try to treat them that way, ok? And just so you know, Doug is along to keep all the travel arrangements straight and because he asked to come. Samuel is a native of Kenya, and even now his wife and children are traveling to the mission to be with him through this month. He is our Kenya expert on cultural expectations and customs, and we will all pay strict attention to what he says. No matter how strange his directions may be, we will follow them: the students, Doug, you, and me. Is that clear?"

Sue was taken aback by Jennie's directness, but answered with a soft, "Very clear." Then louder, "You can count on me, Jennie."

"Good. As we go along I'll give you things to do. In the meantime I'd like you to keep your eye on Alice and Chris. Seems to me we may be having a "trip romance"' blossoming which could mean trouble." Sue nodded. Jennie added, "I'm going back to my seat now. If you have any questions, just ask Samuel or me. And thanks for being cooperative, helpful. This ought to be a great adventure for us all." With that Jennie returned to her seat beside Samuel and the student she had traded with took her place beside Sue who was suddenly a very interactive seat companion.

## 21.

President Clayton smiled with satisfaction. The signed contract lay on the desk in front of him.

He picked up the phone: "Mary, it's a 'go'. Start packing! We start there on February second." After her response he continued with excitement, "No, I haven't told anyone yet, but by day's end all the faculty will know. What an opportunity! Oh, and you can buy new furniture when we get there. We'll sell the old stuff. My raise will make life a lot easier!" He listened, then added, "Someone is walking by whom I want to speak to, so we'll talk later. Love you. Bye."

"Ben, Ben Adkins," he called from the door. "Would you come in here, please?"

Ben almost froze in his tracks. Had someone reported him about his attention to Jennie? But he had tried so hard to avoid breaking the rule. Only Dr. John and Dr. Gene knew. Surely they wouldn't...

The President was walking toward him, smiling broadly. Clayton was still a handsome man. His fifty or so years had been kind to him. Faculty had liked him from his first interview. Maybe that was it, thought Ben: Clayton wanted to quiz him about the morning's faculty decision to fire him.

Falling into step with Ben, Clayton put a friendly arm across his shoulders. "Ben, I have something to tell you, and something to ask you. Let's go inside my office where we can be private."

Ben followed obediently, sitting in the chair the President indicated. He hadn't spoken a word; he didn't dare lest he accuse himself accidentally.

"Ben," President Clayton began, "I have great personal news. Several months ago Mary and I decided our work here was finished. We had raised the endowment, hired good faculty, and increased the student body. It was time to move on before I got any older, so I began to watch for openings on the East coast where Mary's parents and sisters live."

Ben wondered what all this had to do with him. Maybe nothing....

Holding up a sheaf of papers, Clayton continued, "And this is the result. My contract as president of Sheriton University. I had my final interviews over Christmas and I just called Mary to tell her to start packing because we start there February second."

Ben was stunned, but managed to respond, "That's great, President Clayton! And wonderful for Mary. But what will Callegua do? And why are you telling me this before anyone else?"

"Because, Ben, there's going to be an opening at Sheriton in the History Department in the fall, and I want you to join me there. You are tops. The students love you, and didn't I hear you say once that you would love to live on the East coast? You don't have to answer right now, but I want you to give me an answer as soon as you can. You're the person to fill that position, but we have to get your application in right away before someone else is hired. I think they'll hold off hiring until I get there, but I'm not sure. So how about 48 hours? Is that enough time?" Clayton was on the edge of his seat, leaning toward Ben, speaking with excitement that Ben could not ignore.

"You know, sir, that this is a life-changing offer. I don't have a class until later this week, so I'll use the time to make up my mind. Forty-eight hours is tough, but I'll try," Ben replied. "Meanwhile, congratulations. You deserve this step up. I hope it's all you hope for." He stood to leave. The two men shook hands, clapped each other's shoulders, and still in shock, Ben headed to his apartment to think.

Once there he took out a sheet of paper and drew a line down the center. Across the top he put 'Pros' and Cons'. The first word he wrote under

both headings was "Jennie". If he left he could
court her, maybe even this coming semester. But if
he left, he would leave her, perhaps for her to love
someone else. Yet she wanted to go to an East coast
med school, so they would be together after she
graduated. His thoughts were only about her.
Finally, he began to look at Clayton's offer and how
it would affect his career. He was far down the
sheet of paper when the phone rang.

"Ben, have you heard? The faculty chair is
going to give Clayton the bad news today. What a
shock he's in for!"

Ben smiled. "John, you have no idea.
There'll be shock, all right, but not for Clayton."

Dr. John asked, "What are you talking about,
Ben? What do you know that the rest of us don't?"

"Can't say, John. But you'll know before the
day is over. Then we'll talk. Meet you in the
cafeteria at dinner, ok?"

A mystified John clicked off his cell phone,
then immediately called Gene and invited him to
dinner with, "Ben knows something we don't.
You've gotta be there!"

At the end of the day everyone knew about
the President moving to the East coast university,
ending the need to tell him Callegua was about to
fire him     .

Only John and Gene knew about Ben.

### 22.

"Sue! I'd know you anywhere!" exclaimed
Trisha as the group clambered down the steps from
the plane. "And you must be Jennie. You look so
much like your mother!" Trisha was excited and
fearful at the same time. In the city she had learned
of many villages being burned, some close to her

mission, and now she was not sure it was safe for the group to be in Kenya. But there was no turning back. Suddenly a tall dark man was standing in front of her. This must be Samuel, she thought.

Miss Trisha," Samuel spoke excitedly, "did my wife and children come with you?"

"Sorry, Samuel, but there just wasn't room for all the students and them too." Trisha hoped God would forgive her lie. She didn't have the heart to tell him they hadn't arrived yet; maybe they would be there by the time the group arrived.

Samuel nodded his head, but stepped to the side of the group. This was a huge disappointment. He had dreamed of this moment, of taking Zaporra in his arms, of hugging his children and showing them off to the group. Now he must wait again.

Meanwhile everyone was clearing customs, getting their passports stamped, and finding their way to the two busses waiting for them. This was the first cultural shock: the busses were old, the seats torn, and when they began to travel it was clear that the springs in the seats and underneath the buses had long since given out. Some took it as great fun, but some grew very quiet, wondering what they had gotten themselves into. Bouncing on the dirt and gravel roads made the trip to the mission seem longer than it was so that a shout of joy went up when the first buildings came into sight. But no one was more excited than Samuel.

Trisha asked everyone to stay on the bus while she got the list of each person's room number, so there was some order right from the beginning. As she stepped off the first bus, Samuel came running from the second bus. "Where are they, Miss Trisha? Where is my family?"

"Come with me, Samuel, and we'll see if they're in their room." Trisha pointed to number 24, the only guest room large enough for a family.

Samuel took off running, flung open the door and stared into the empty room. "Miss Trisha," he cried out, "they're not here!"

"Oh, Samuel, I'm so sorry. The truth is they haven't arrived yet. I had hoped they would be here by the time we returned from the airport. We've been watching the roads for them every day. I do hope they're safe. The rebels have been burning villages closer and closer to us. I'm not even sure it's all right for the Callegua group to be here. We'll have to be on alert every minute."

"Miss Trisha, does the mission have a car I can use? I must go look for my wife and my children. I trust God they are safe, but they maybe have to hide a lot."

Trisha saw the anguish on Samuel's face. The mission had one four-wheel drive Land Rover, the only car that could survive the dirt roads. If they lost that car....

"Of course, Samuel." Trisha reached into her pocket and pulled out a large key ring, removed the key for the Land Rover, and handing it to Samuel added, "There is only one road from here toward your village." She pointed toward what looked like a narrow rutted path. "It is there. God go with you, Samuel, and may you find your family quickly."

The last words were spoken into the wind. Samuel was already behind the wheel and moving out onto the road. His very soul was filled with alarm: His Zaporra, Paul and Lydia, hiding from evil rebels! "Oh God! Protect them!" was his cry. This was nothing like driving the roads in America where he had learned. Here he had to dodge huge ruts, sometimes guessing where the road was. He passed a village in ruins, the smoke still rising from an attack. His stomach lurched when he realized that the large pile still burning was people. He saw no one alive.

Suddenly, in the midst of his fear and distress, he heard a voice. Or was it just in his head? "Be still, Samuel. I am in charge. Your Zaporra and children are safe and just a few miles ahead." He looked around to see who had spoken, but there was no one. Had God spoken to him? He was strangely at peace. Calm. Assured. He slowed the Land Rover now, looking carefully from side to side. He did not call out, lest the rebels were still around and might attack him. The sun was getting low in the sky; soon he would not be able to see, and he had no flashlight with him. Almost in a whisper he would breathe, "Zaporra, Zaporra!"

As he rounded a turn in the road he thought he saw a woman run into the tall elephant grass. Drawing up to the spot, he turned off the engine, stepped out of the Land Rover so he could be seen, and spoke loudly, "I am Samuel come to rescue you." Then he waited. Finally, when he was about to give up, a woman stepped out of the grass. "Samuel? Is it really you?"

"Zaporra? Is it really you?" was his gasped reply.

She fairly flew into his arms, but the embrace was brief as he pushed her back. "But where are the children, Paul and Lydia?" Samuel's voice was full of distress.

"I have them hidden in the tall grass." Zaporra called over her shoulder as she ran to get their children, with Samuel at her heels.

"Children, this is your father come to rescue us. Come quickly, and be very quiet." They were crouched near the road but completely hidden. Samuel swept both of them into his arms and swiftly he and Zaporra broke through the grasses and climbed into the Land Rover. Everything happened so fast that the children had no time to resist this stranger that had just entered their lives, had saved them from the rebels that were roaming throughout Kenya, killing and burning as they went.

It was a happy couple that pulled into the mission yard. The Callegua students swarmed around the Rover, greeting Zaporra, making much ado about Paul and Lydia who had never seen so many white people in their young lives. They were as curious about the students as the students were about them. Both Paul and Lydia clung to their mother, not knowing whether to be happy or afraid. Paul was beginning to remember his father, but Lydia was afraid of this big, strange man.

"Let us have some time alone," begged Samuel. "We will join you at dinner time, but right now we need to get acquainted again." With that he led Zaporra, Paul and Lydia, to the quarters Trisha had shown him earlier.

Meanwhile each of the students had been assigned six to a room, had unpacked and reported to the central room that was used for dining, school, meetings, and indoor play when it rained. Trisha had handed out work project lists. Doug and Jennie had assigned students to fit the jobs. David Belkin's cold was worse, so much so that to his sorrow he was sent to the infirmary to be kept away from everyone. Any romantic ideas he had about Jennie were quickly fading.

A simple dinner was served, followed by prayer and a New Testament reading from the book of James, reminding them that faith that does nothing is useless. Then everyone was sent to their quarters and admonished to go to sleep quickly because the day would start early. Sue, assigned to room with the two faculty members and Jennie, wanted to talk, but Jennie turned her head to the wall and was soon sound asleep. Sue opened the door to discover that all was quite suddenly dark, so she reluctantly climbed into bed, realized she was exhausted, and was asleep in minutes. In the middle of the night she sat straight up in bed. What had she heard? Just the strange place, she decided, and rolled over to sleep again.

Samuel and Zaporra also heard the sound of soft footsteps and whispered words. They held each other tightly and listened long into the night.

Trisha slept fitfully, wondering if she had done the right thing bringing these students into Kenya when there was so much danger. Once she was disturbed by an unidentifiable sound: "God, help me to remember you're in charge," she prayed, and then sank into an exhausted sleep.

## 23.

The next morning everyone was excited to meet the children whose pictures they had received the previous semester. It was noisy and joyful in the meeting room. Jennie picked out Daniel and Priscilla right away: they looked just like the pictures she had posted above her desk on campus. The morning was gone too soon with laughter and play, but the promise of a whole month made a happy goodbye after lunch as the children returned to their classrooms.

The team, however, quickly divided into their units, following directions from the mission's foreman, Peter. He was a sturdy, family man, whose wife oversaw the kitchen. Together they kept track of the mission supplies and made sure everything ran smoothly. Peter soon had some students painting walls, others doing repairs on buildings, while still others helped in the mission office preparing government forms under Trisha's supervision. Two students were good mechanics and were assigned to repair the two mission farm tractors and teach the Kenyan volunteers how to do mechanical work.

The first two weeks flew by: children in the early morning, work assignments from mid-morning until late afternoon, and play time until dinner. David Belkin soon recovered and became the group chaplain, plus holding Bible classes for the Kenyans who came to the mission.

Trisha was absolutely thrilled with the progress the group was making. Even Sue had found a niche; she was teaching the Kenyan women how to use the old Singer treadle machine that had sat unused for years. The fine clothes in Sue's suitcase became fabric to make into children's clothes. The women laughed at Sue's dresses, but soon began to cut them apart to make patchwork or blended fabric designs. Sue was glad her grandmother had taught her to sew.

Doug had begun to be everywhere Jennie was. Often, they sat together and shared their lifegoals. Jennie found him very appealing, even someone she could spend her life with. He was clearly falling in love with her but respected the distance she needed as leader of the group. Her desire to be a doctor did not faze him. He wasn't ready to settle into marriage now. He could afford to wait a few years. It was okay with Doug to take it easy, to go slow.

As the month moved on Samuel began to take the Land Rover into the countryside. The footsteps that had awakened him the first night bothered him enough that he was always looking for evidence that the rebels might have plans to destroy the mission. After all, it was a Christian mission, and therefore a target. With a couple of the Callegua boys and some Kenyan volunteers a fire fighting water system had been developed as a safeguard against rebel burning. At mid-month it covered all but two

of the twelve mission complex buildings and they
were working very hard to complete the system
before month's end.

## 24.

After the first week, Alice Dakin and Chris
Conrad had agreed to meet every afternoon after
rest time. They would take their Kenyan children
off to the edge of the compound and teach them
games and songs. The weather was cooperating –
not too hot with only occasional rain – so this
playtime was special for the six of them. After they
returned the children to their quarters to get ready
for dinner, the two would walk hand-in-hand, every
day falling a little more in love. Lasting love, they
thought, and this Kenya experience was something
they would always share.

One afternoon, engrossed in conversation,
they suddenly realized that they had walked beyond
the mission compound; in fact the path had almost
disappeared, hidden by the tall switch grass that
closed in behind them as they walked. The mission
was nowhere in sight: nothing looked familiar at all.
They were completely lost.

Chris checked his watch. It was almost
dinnertime. They would be missed and someone
would come looking for them. Meantime,
concerned about the sudden darkness that ended the
Kenyan day, they tried to retrace their steps to find
the path amidst the grass.

"Chris, it all looks the same to me," Alice's
voice trembled slightly. "Are you sure we're going
in the right direction?" They had been told almost
daily not to leave the compound. What would the
others think?

Chris, catching Alice's fear, answered in as
strong a voice as he could muster. "These trees

look right to me. I think we passed them before."
Actually he had been so intent on Alice that he had
barely noticed their surroundings, which is how
they had become lost in the first place. He scanned
the horizon. Why couldn't he see the rooftops of
the mission buildings? Surely they hadn't walked
so far away.

"Okay. Let's choose a tree and walk toward
it, then we'll choose another and another to keep us
in a straight line until we come across a road or a
path. That way we won't go in a circle." Chris
wished now he had paid more attention in Boy
Scouts. He wasn't at all sure this was the right
thing to do. To Alice he added, "And we must walk
quickly. You know how dark the night is."

Alice shivered at the thought of being in the
Kenyan night alone. In the elephant grass she heard
a grunting sound; was that a wild boar? Or the
muffled sound of an animal feasting on its kill?
Animals! They would be all around them in the
night. What if they were attacked? What would
they do? They had nothing: no flashlight, no
jackets, and no water. Her mind traveled as fast as
her feet as they hurried from tree to tree with no
sign of the mission anywhere.

"Stop!" A tall, sinewy dark man rose up out
of the grass. A bandana covered part of his face, but
his drug-laden bloodshot eyes burrowed into their
very souls. Slung over his shoulder was an AK-47.
A canteen hung from a belt around his waist, and
the hunting knife beside it could kill animal or
human. Chris was sure it had killed both.

"You!" He pointed at Chris. "Over there.
Sit." Chris quickly moved, sitting on the ground
where the man directed him.

Alice began to shake uncontrollably. She had
read horror stories of the rebels raping the women,

cutting them apart, or burning them alive. The man stepped close to her.

"Why do you shake so, white one? Do you fear me?"

She did not answer.

"You should. You could be dead soon by this knife." He pulled it from its sheath and ran it under her chin. When she pulled back, he laughed a rough, coarse laugh.

"What is your name?" Chris found his voice. Maybe he could distract the man away from Alice.

Spittle landed on Chris's nose and slid over his lips. "You do not need to know," was the reply.

Undaunted, Chris asked, "What are you fighting for?"

"We are destroying the evil government who takes away our land, "was the bitter answer. He was proud of his purpose.

"But why do you destroy your own people, burn their houses, kill the women and children?" Chris had his attention now.

"Because they support the government, so they are evil too." The rebel shifted uneasily.

Chris pushed on: "But killing, murdering, burning – that is evil also. You are using evil to fight evil."

Suddenly the knife was at Chris's neck. "You say too much. We follow our leader. He isright." Then the man added, "On your feet!"

Chris scrambled to obey. "What are you going to do with us? We have nothing to do with your government. We are Americans."

Startled, the rebel drew back a step. Americans had money. He would be an important man if he brought these two back to the camp. They could hold them for ransom.... and the others would enjoy this pretty little white girl.

Swiftly he bound their hands with the grass he expertly twisted into a sharp-edged cord, tying it tight enough to draw blood. Then he fastened them together. Alice began to cry softly. In her mind she was praying: "Oh God, deliver us."

"Quiet!" the rebel demanded, as he swung his AK around and, prodding them cruely with it. "Move!"

They walked slowly, stumbling as they tried to move together. Chris began to pray in a whisper, "Oh God, through the power of your Son, Jesus Christ, we claim your promise of deliverance. We will not fear for we know you are with us. We thank you for the salvation you brought to this earth, and we pray for this man who is your child, that he may come to know you and have his spirit cleansed and set free. We pray for deliverance, but we are willing to be used in whatever way you choose. In the name and power of Jesus we pray." Together he and Alice said, "Amen."

Suddenly the man stopped, then without a word disappeared into the grass. They heard a growing commotion in the distance: whistles, voices calling their names, a car horn blaring. Then silence.

"Here! Over here!" Chris whistled loudly through his teeth and together they screamed, "Help! Help! We're here!"

They moved as fast as they could toward the voices that had begun calling again. "They didn't hear us, Chris. We have to scream louder." Alice's voice was desperate. They must be found before the searchers left to look in another place.

Again came the silence. This time Chris and Alice called out with their loudest shouts. The car horn answered, then was quiet. They shouted again: "Here! Here!"

Chris had never seen such a beautiful Land Rover. Old, battered, but beautiful. They had been found. They were safe. They had been delivered.

A very somber group gathered in the meeting room that night to hear their story. Chris and Alice were symbols of what could happen to anyone in this cruel country. They praised God for keeping Chris and Alice safe, and prayed for Trisha and her helpers and the precious children.

It was late when the meeting broke up. Trisha had put extra people on security: she knew the rebels would be angry they had lost a potential ransom. The team had accomplished much, but she was glad they would be leaving in two days. As for herself, she would stay until God called her elsewhere. After all, she had children to look after. With that renewed commitment, Trisha went peacefully to sleep.

**25.**

The last day was set aside for parties. Jennie opened her duffle bag of gifts to the thrilled amazement of Priscilla and Daniel. The three of them had bonded so that the separation was hard: the gifts softened the parting. It was not just Jennie, but each of the students was distressed to leave this place that had changed their view of the world. Tears fell on many pillows that night. Sleep was hard to come by.

Next morning the old buses were reluctantly loaded for the trip to the airport after hugs and prayers and songs with the children. Trisha put Peter, her trusted foreman, in charge of the mission, and joined the group on the bus for the long bumpy ride. She sat down next to Sue.

"Sue, thank you for coming. It is wonderful to know you again, but as a different person. Our

freshman year at Callegua is long gone and I do
hope we can be friends for the rest of our lives."

Sue's eyes flooded with tears. They ran down
her cheeks so that it was difficult for her to respond.

Finally she stammered, "Trisha.... Your work
here.... your dedication.... your faith.... well, I
haven't told anyone else, but this week after chapel
I asked God to forgive my past.... and....I.... I've
become a real Christian for the first time in my
life."
Now it was Trisha's turn to weep. "Oh Sue! How
wonderful! God has answered my prayers for you!
We will be real sisters in Christ," Trish exulted.
"But Sue, you must tell the group. What a
wonderful testimony it will be for them."

"Tell the group? I.... I'm not sure I can do
that," Sue returned.

"Sure you can. Just stand up, right here on the
bus, and tell them how this trip has changed you."

No one could have been more surprised than
Doug to hear his mother's confession of faith. The
students cheered and clapped for her. Then they
began to stand up and tell their stories, so that by
the time they reached the airport it was a happy
group that Trisha waved good-bye to, and Jennie
knew the trip had transformed lives and would soon
affect Callegua University and all its students.

Samuel's Zaporra, Paul and Lydia, were
staying at the mission until he came home in July,
giving him much peace. Coming back to Kenya
had assured him it was where he wanted to spend
his life after graduation.

David Belkin was more convinced of his
calling, but now was also thinking about serving on
the mission field. He also knew that Jennie was not
the life partner he had thought. She would never be
submissive to him. For that matter he had to admit

she had scarcely given him a second look, so focused was she on her leadership of the group. No, the truth was, she was just too independent for his liking. Meghan popped into his thoughts.... Yes, he would have to get acquainted with her when they got back to campus.

Trisha arrived back at the mission about twilight. All her workers were waiting for her, some wailing loudly. As she stepped off the bus Peter stepped forward: "Oh, Miss Trisha, something terrible has happened. Some men came and tried to burn our buildings, but we stopped them with our water system; we even ran them off by turning the hoses on them. But one building is gone: our storeroom, our supplies. We did the best we could, but now what are we going to do?"

Trisha had dreamed a dream filled with fire just a few nights before. Now it had happened. But she had also heard a voice of assurance in her dream, and with perfect calm she spoke to all of them. "Do not worry, dear friends. God will provide all our needs. We will rebuild the storeroom, and God will fill it."

With that she thanked them all for saving the mission and suggested they go to their quarters to rest. As she walked to her own room, she remembered Sue's last words to her: "Now Trisha, I have money. If you need anything, anything at all, just email me and if money can solve the need, it will be yours the next day."

Amazing. Sue would save her. Who would have thought that would ever happen? God was indeed in charge. Help was just an email away.

## 26.

Jennie stared out the airplane window at the

sea of clouds beneath her. Something wasn't quite right. Doug was sitting beside her with a strange valise tucked under the seat in front of him. In the airport a well-dressed man had approached Doug, handed him the valise full of business papers and contracts for his father, and told him to be sure to ask for Mr. Azizz and go through his security check line.

Jennie interrupted Doug's reading: "Doug, who was that man who gave you the valise?"

"I don't know. He said he was a business partner of my father's. Dad told me at Christmas that one of his partners would meet us at the airport with contracts for him and it would be much simpler if I just brought them home rather than depend on the mail – which isn't always dependable!" He flashed a smile at Jennie, glad to sit by her on this long flight. He'd have to thank his secretary when he got back for making that seating change.

"Have you opened it? Do you know what's in it?" Jennie queried.

"No, it has a code lock. That's why he told me to go to Mr. Azizz: he knew the lock. Funny thing, though, he didn't bother to open it. Said he knew what was in it and just waved me through."

"What's your dad's business, Doug?" Fear was beginning to creep into Jennie's thinking.

"I don't really know. He never discussed it with any of us. When we asked, he would laugh and say our inheritance was safe, not to worry. Then he always changed the subject. I don't think even Mom knows what he does. I heard him tell her one day not to worry 'her pretty little head' as long as there was plenty of money coming in. Then he'd buy her an expensive present to convince her there was plenty more money where that came from. But I admit, I've wondered." Doug was quiet for a couple of minutes. Then he added, "Why do you ask?"

"Did you see the two men who got on the plane when we did? One of them was in line in front of you and one behind you. And they're sitting on the plane that way: one—see a couple of rows ahead? —is sitting in front of the group, and the other is behind all of us. I think they're watching you."

"Don't be silly, Jennie. Why would anyone watch me?"

"I don't know, Doug, but I think it has something to do with that valise. Why don't you check out my suspicions? Get up and go to the restroom. See if one of them follows you."

"Okay, but I think you're imagining things." Doug stood up, walked toward the back of the plane, and waited outside the occupied lavatories. The man at the back of the group followed him down the aisle. Deciding to take matters into his own hands, Doug said, "Long flight, isn't it?"

"I've been on longer."

Doug was determined to start a conversation. "Do you fly a lot? I'm a travel agent based in Florida. Maybe I could help you with your travel arrangements."

"No thanks," was the taciturn answer. "My office takes care of that." Then he added, "Of course it might be possible that I need your help sometime. Do you have a business card?"

"Sure." Doug pulled his wallet out of his front pants pocket, drew out a card, and handed it to the man, who examined it carefully.

"Doug Williams," he read. "Any relation to J.W. Williams of Ohio?" And before Doug could respond, the man added, "But that's pretty absurd, isn't it?"

"Not at all," was Doug's reply. "J.W.'s my dad. Guess you know him through football. He was quite a player in college. Callegua College, now University. Sends them a lot of money, too. Good man, my dad." At that moment one of the lavatory doors opened and Doug had to enter it. When he came out the man was back in his seat, but he nodded to Doug as Doug walked up the aisle.

"Well," said Jennie, "he followed you, didn't he?"

"Yeah, but once I got him talking he was a pretty nice guy. Knew my dad; how's that for a coincidence? I gave him my card, offered to do travel arrangements for him. I think you're on the wrong track, Jennie."

"Maybe so." Jennie wasn't convinced. How naive Doug was to give the man his card. Then, changing the subject, she added, "Oh look-- they're serving dinner," and dropped the subject.

When the group finally landed in Chicago and cleared customs, Jennie noted with relief that the two suspicious men were far ahead of them going toward the baggage area. Doug caught sight of his dad and sprinted ahead to greet him. "Here's the valise, dad, just like you asked."

"Good job, son," J.W. said, taking the bag. "A real help to me. Where's your mother?"

Jennie stood by, watching Doug and his dad, while the group moved off. Only she saw the valise move from one to the other.

As Doug turned to look for his mother, the two men from the plane stepped up on either side of J.W. "You're under arrest, Mr. Williams. FBI." They flashed their badges, then added, "and we'll take the valise." With that, one took the bag and the other pulled J.W.'s arms around behind his back and handcuffed him.

"What are you doing?" J. W. retorted. "You can't do this to me! That valise contains my business contracts, and I need them. Let me go immediately!"

Sue walked up just then, saw her husband in handcuffs, and heard one of the men say, "FBI. We've been waiting a long time to catch up with you. I think we can finally quit waiting." With that they led J.W. off to a room in the airport. As they walked away, one turned to Doug and said, "Stay close to home. We'll want to question you."

Sue saw the arrest in shock. "Doug, do you know what this is about... your father?"

Doug was as surprised and stunned as Sue. "I haven't a clue, Mom. All I know is that they were eager to get that valise Dad had me pick up."

"What will we do?" Sue still hadn't moved.

"I guess we'll collect our baggage and join the group as if nothing had happened. Then we'll wait to find out about Dad's arrest."

Jennie, standing nearby, saw and heard everything. Doug and Sue had her to thank that the group was swiftly steered away from the two of them and into the baggage reclaim area. The Callegua bus was waiting. For Jennie it was a welcome sight. She was almost home; she had so much to tell her mother. One thing was sure: she didn't need Doug in her life as anything more than a good friend. She was the last one on the bus. Samuel had checked to see that each student had boarded with his or her luggage, so with a grateful heart Jennie sank into her seat.

The Kenya trip was over and she was glad it was.

## 27.

Dr. Adkins looked on approvingly as the

Kenya group entered the gym auditorium. The
Student Body Council had arranged a grand
reception to welcome the mission group back, and
as they came through the door, a shout and applause
greeted them. This turned into a foot-stomping roar
when Samuel and Jennie entered. Ben felt his
stomach tighten, his heart speed up, when he saw
Jennie. Nothing had changed. If anything, he
yearned for her more. She was tired and slightly
disheveled, but to Ben, more beautiful than ever.
No doubt. She was the woman he wanted in his life
forever.

Jennie was swept into the crowd of interim
students and up onto the stage at the far end of the
gym where many of the faculty members stood.
The faculty chair stepped to the mike: "Most of you
students know, but our Kenya group probably does
not know that President Clayton has left Callegua to
become the president of Sheriton University on the
East Coast, so here to welcome you back properly,
is our interim president, Dr. Ingram." With that the
head of the Engineering Department stepped to the
mike and continued the greeting. A small shiver
went through Jennie. This man was known as an
ultra-conservative in politics and religion; he
couldn't possibly be good for Callegua.

At that moment Ben Adkins caught Jennie's
eye, smiled broadly at her, and mouthed a
"welcome back" with his lips. What should have
been a moment of triumph as she was called to the
stage was instead a mix of emotions and confusion.
Now she was sure he was bent on harassing her.
This very week she would march into his office and
let him know to back off!

Her thoughts were broken by the words of the
president: "And to honor each student and their
student leaders, the University is giving them each a
free meal ticket for the spring semester."

A cheer went up in the gym. The group that had gathered on the stage jumped up and down, clapping with joy. This was no small gift, and completely unexpected. Jennie, ever in control, shook hands with the president and thanked him for the generosity of the school, and said she hoped the group would contribute in many ways from their experiences during the new semester. In the crowd, Ben beamed with pride at her composure.

He would have liked to walk her back to her dorm after the reception ended, but he had not yet heard from Sheriton U about the history appointment. President Clayton was gone, and he was on his own: not the time to get dismissed for fraternization with a student. But soon, perhaps, soon. It was enough that Jennie was back where he could see her again.

## 28.

Another story was unfolding for Sue and Doug. Sent home by the FBI, they arrived to find the house surrounded. With cold courtesy they were presented with a search warrant. Instructing Sue and Doug to wait in the living room, they went through J.W.'s files, confiscated his computer and cell phone, searched his closet and dresser drawers. A safe was found tucked away in the basement that neither Sue nor Doug knew was there. The lock's combination turned up deep in a file cabinet: the safe was filled with stacks of money. Doug and Sue were amazed. Then one of the searchers called out, "I've got it!" The others crowded around him, looking at the paper he had in his hand. "That's it," said the man who seemed to be in charge. "We can go now," and with those words they gathered up everything and left, telling Sue and Doug, "Don't leave. We'll be back."

Alone at last, Doug advised a bewildered Sue to call their lawyer, then changed his mind and said instead, "Get a new lawyer. For all we know, the lawyer you and Dad have had for years knows all about this. He may be someone we'll want for a witness. And Mom, if you've got money or things that Dad didn't buy you, like the jewelry from Grandma, you need to get busy and identify everything. If my guess is right, Dad was running drugs. If this is the case, the FBI will want everything that came from the drug money, which is just about everything you have, including the house."

Sue, realizing the enormity of the situation, burst into tears. Doug waited until her tears had stopped, then said, "Mom, I'll stick around for a couple of weeks to help you. We'll get through this thing together. Should we call Laina? They'll probably track her down, too."

Controlled now, Sue thanked Doug for his offer, then added, "Before we do anything, Doug, there's one thing we must do."

"What's that, Mom?"

"Pray. Pray that God will guide us through this terrible time, will give us calm and courage... and peace."

"You'll have to do it, Mom. I don't know how," was Doug's reply.

Minutes later it was a calm twosome who sat at the kitchen table, armed with a cup of tea and pen and paper, to begin to separate Sue's life from J.W.'s.

## 29.

In Hollywood Laina was just walking onto the set, prepared for a long day of filming. The director hoped to get three episodes done each day this week so everyone could take a week off around Easter, so Laina had been frantically learning lines. So far he seemed pleased with her performance and she didn't want to blow this incredible opportunity.

As she entered the huge sound stage, she saw two men arguing with the director. Coming closer she heard him say, "But you can't take her! Do you have any idea how much it costs to shut down production? All the people who will lose work? She's in every episode! Please!"

Other cast members were standing off to one side where Laina joined them. "What's up?" she asked.

"You tell us. It's you they're arguing about," came the response.

"Me? What are you saying? Who are those men?"

"FBI. You must have messed up bad," someone said, then added, "Are you doing drugs? I heard that word, drugs."

Laina was stunned. When she decided to become an actress, she took a vow never to touch drugs or alcohol. Her friend Judy committed suicide while she was high, and every day it seemed some actor or actress was arrested for drugs or a DUI.

"Laina – over here," called the director. When she had joined him and the two strangers, he continued: "These men want to question you – FBI -- They were going to take you to their headquarters but they've agreed to use my office so we can get on with the shoot. We'll hold your scenes till after they've finished."

He paused. Of all the actors on the show, Laina was the last one he expected to bring trouble. He liked her innocence. As he walked away to start

the day, he called over his shoulder, "Good luck!"
From what the FBI men had told him, she was
going to need it.

Once in the director's office, the men helped
themselves to his newly brewed coffee, offered
some to Laina which she refused, and began with
"What do you know about your dad's business?"

"His business?" Laina answered
incredulously. "Nothing at all."

"So tell us, Miss Williams, when were you
home last?" They already knew but wanted to test
her honesty.

"Thanksgiving. I was too busy to go home at
Christmas," she began. "But wait. What is your
purpose? If you're going to interrogate me, I need
to know what's going on – and I need to make a
phone call."

"Easy, miss. We're not taking you off to jail.
We just want to talk to you," came the reply.

Laina had begun to realize her situation.
Something serious had happened at home and she
needed to know about it before anything she said
might affect her dad. She had watched enough TV
to know she could make a phone call or have a
lawyer with her, so she answered the man as calmly
as she could: "I'll be glad to talk to you when my
lawyer is present."

The men bristled. They thought she would be
a pushover, that they could get her to talk without
any trouble. But Laina was smart, and she certainly
wasn't going to betray her family, whatever was
going on.

"All right. Get your lawyer. We'll be back
tomorrow. But don't leave town. We'll know
where you are. You'll get a call tonight to set up
tomorrow's meeting." With that they left the office.

When she was sure they were gone, Laina
picked up the office phone. "Doug? What's going

on? Why are you home? When did you get back from Africa? Are you and Mom okay?" The questions tumbled out nonstop.

"Whoa! Slow down, Sis," answered Doug. "First, how do you know something's going on?"

"The FBI was waiting for me at work when I got here this morning, wanting to know about Dad's business. What's that all about? Is it drugs?" Laina still couldn't believe her own words.

"I'll tell you about that later, from your cell phone. Did you talk to them?" Doug wondered what Laina knew. Probably nothing, but she and her Dad were really close. Maybe that's part of why she went to Hollywood. Maybe Dad was using her like he had apparently used him.

He shook the thought away as he heard Laina's answer.

"I only answered a couple of questions and then told them I wouldn't be interrogated without my lawyer present. Look – hang up and I'll call your cell from mine in case your line is tapped. Give me five minutes."

Laina hung up, told the director she would be back in ten minutes or so, then went out to the parking lot where, in her naiveté, she thought no one could pick up her cell call. Actually the FBI men were listening from an unmarked car just a few parking spaces from where she stood to call Doug. They even could see her facial expressions as he told her all that had happened.

Laina was stunned. Her father, J.W. Williams, generous, upright citizen and wonderful dad: her father suspected of being the mastermind of a huge illegal business? Finally she stopped Doug to ask the question that bothered her even more: "Doug, what about Mom? Did she know?"

"Are you kidding? She's in shock. Besides the deceit, she stands to lose everything: her husband, the house, everything bought with Dad's business money – and she could be named an accomplice and go to prison. No, she's totally innocent. You should have seen her face when they found the second safe stuffed with money! Total bewilderment. And she keeps saying that Dad never changed. That he did it to her in college and now he's ruined her again. What's that all about?" Doug still didn't know all the details of why his mother had left Callegua College in her freshman year.

"Not important now, bro. Look, I have to go back to work. Keep me posted. The FBI guys are supposed to call tonight to set a meeting time, so I have to get a lawyer on board."

They agreed to keep each other informed as soon as anything happened. The call ended, Laina went back inside, stepped onto the set and into her role, thankful that she had studied her lines. Remembering them kept her from thinking about the disaster that had just hit her family, but way down in her subconscious she knew that nothing would ever be the same.

Outside an unmarked black car rolled quietly out of the parking lot. The driver turned to the passenger and said simply, "Tomorrow," then wheeled into traffic and the two disappeared.

### 30.

Back on campus, Jennie handed over to Samuel the responsibility for the team, repaying Callegua's investment by scheduling speakers to various groups on and off campus. Everyone wanted to hear about their adventures and the children, plus Trish had emailed them about the buildings that were burned. The students wanted to raise money to help replace them. Samuel was eager to help out his country any way he could. Now he feared for the safety of his family staying at the mission.

With Samuel in charge, Jennie turned to focus on her studies, spending almost every spare moment in the library. She knew her grade point average (GPA) would be a deciding factor in her acceptance to med school. By mid-February she had her applications in to Harvard and Boston on the East Coast, and Stanford in California. She was grateful that her full scholarship would pay for whatever university she wanted to go to, but it was hard to wait for their responses.

"Jennie.... Jennie Reyes?" A male voice broke her concentration, and the silence of the library so that the other students turned to look. A tall, slender young man dressed completely in black was the speaker. Dark wavy hair dropped over his forehead; his dark eyes danced with intelligence. When Jennie turned toward him he smiled, revealing perfectly even white teeth. She caught her breath just looking at this handsome stranger. She had to swallow hard before she could answer, "Yes, I'm Jennie Reyes."

He flashed a badge. "FBI. I need to talk with you. But not here," he added, realizing the whole room was watching them. "Would you mind taking a walk with me. This needs to be a private conversation."

"Of course," was her answer, though she was mystified. What did the FBI have to do with her? Maybe this was a background check for Harvard or Boston – or Stanford. She'd heard that nobody trusted anyone in California.

Carefully marking her place in her reading, Jennie rose, suddenly aware of being short: she barely came to his shoulder. And her hair! She brushed back the bangs that were growing out, while wishing she had put on better jeans that morning.

"Where can we go where we won't be observed?" he asked as the library doors closed silently behind them.

"Down by the lake is a bench hidden by some bushes. Would that do?" Jennie didn't bother to add that it was a favorite spot for couples late at night.

"Sounds great. Take us there." His voice was full of authority, like he was used to being in charge. Jennie liked it. She liked him, she decided.

They walked quickly across campus, Jennie taking a route behind most of the buildings to stay out of sight. It was as they walked between two buildings that Ben Adkins saw them and was suddenly filled with jealousy. Who was that with Jennie? She was his girl, not this stranger's. Even at a distance he could see the worshipful look on Jennie's face when she looked at this man. Where were they going? What were they up to? Ben decided he had to follow them, although he was on his way to a student appointment. He'd make his excuses later.

"My name is Riley," the stranger began when they reached the bench and sat down. "Riley Singer. Funny name for an FBI agent when part of my job is to make people 'sing', so to speak. And I know you want to know what's up, so I'll get right to it." He flashed his electric smile, and continued: "What do you know about Doug Kronen?"

So that was it! Jennie relaxed, shook her head negatively, and said, "Not much. He was on our trip to Kenya last month and we had friendly conversation. Nothing of substance. Why?" Remembering the incident at the airport she thought she knew why, but waited for Riley's answer.

"His Dad is under arrest and we have to interview everyone who might tell us if the son and daughter are involved in his probably illegal business. Also Sue, the mother. We're pretty sure she's innocent, shocked by the whole thing, but the son has a good cover with his travel business in Florida. That's a natural for his business in both the U.S. and Cuba. Then the daughter works in L.A., a natural business center. It may just be happenstance that they're located where they are, but we've got to be sure. And what do you know about the valise Doug carried for his father?"

"The only thing I know about the sister is her name, Laina, and that she's an actress. I can't help you much there. Doug I know a little better, but if you want my judgment, he is innocent. That valise he brought from Kenya? His dad told him it was business papers too important to trust to the mail. On the plane I thought he was being followed, but he laughed at the idea, even innocently gave his business card to one of your men so he could help him with future travel. And no one could have been more startled than Doug when his dad was handcuffed and taken away at the airport. I think, in your terms, he's totally 'clean.'"

"And his mother, Sue?"

"She was a roommate of my mother's in the 70's here at Callegua. Doug invited her to go on the trip as a chaperone and she worked very well with the group. That's really all I know about her."

Riley was impressed with Jennie. She was not only beautiful but obviously intelligent, just the kind of girl he'd been looking for. But any thoughts of that kind had to be held in check: she might end up a witness in this case. But he couldn't resist turning the conversation a little personal.

"What are you studying? Teaching? Good

career for a woman."

The spell was broken. Whatever attraction Jennie felt toward Riley was shattered at this derogatory question, so classic coming from a man.

And he knew he had stumbled by the coolness of her answer: "I hope to go to Harvard Medical School when I graduate. Now, is this conversation finished?" She stood to leave.

"Only to say that we may call on you again." His voice was suddenly formal. Obviously Jennie had decided the interview was over. "It would probably be good if we took different paths across campus. Nice talking to you." He reached out to shake Jennie's hand. The soft hand but firm handshake told him that he had passed up a great opportunity. Med school, he thought, mentally kicking himself as he drove away for being so stupid.

Ben Adkins was relieved as he watched Jennie walk back to the library alone. From his hiding place he had heard enough of the conversation to know this was not a romance. Then he was embarrassed at how his obsession with Jennie had forced him to hide like a small boy listening at a keyhole. It was time to put this out in the open. He would take her off campus for dinner, very soon.

Later, Jennie's new cell phone rang as she was on her way to chemistry class.

"Jennie?" her mother asked. "I've just had a visit from the FBI, wanting to know about J.W. Williams. What a surprise after all these years. Do you know why they wanted to talk to me?"

Jennie had put off calling her mother, hoping she wouldn't get dragged into this situation, so now she gave her a hurried account of what had happened coming back from Kenya, adding, "but I can't talk any more, Mom. My chem class is about to begin. Later, ok? Love you!" and shut off her phone.

Joan stood in her office staring at the silent phone. J.W. …. what kind of business would the FBI care about? Poor Sue…. I wonder why Sue married J.W. after what he did to her in college?….. And now this. Joan reached for the list of team members and phone numbers Jennie had given her. The least she could do was call Sue and sympathize with her. Strange, after all these years…

.

## 31.

The campus was quiet during Easter week. Most of the students had gone home or off to celebrate Easter break. Meghan Kronen was not one of them. She didn't want to go home to face her parents again, and she didn't have enough money to go anywhere else, thanks to her dad's failing business. And this morning she was preoccupied with the calendar. This was the second month she had missed her period. That fling she had in January…. she couldn't even remember the guy's name…. just a one-time thing when she felt desperate for sex and he was available. Surely she wasn't pregnant! At least her mother was engaged when she got pregnant in college….

And what would she tell David?

When the Kenya team came back to campus at the end of January, David Belkin had asked her to go with him to the Junior Class play. Even though he intended to be a minister, which was a real put-off, he had a great sense of humor and was fun to be with. That date led to another and another and soon they were an 'item' on campus.

Meghan was in real conflict. She realized she was falling in love with David. Together they shared her strong views on abortion and he helped her get the Pro-Life Club up and running well. But she hadn't told David about her rebellion from her parents, the night of drinking, or the casual sex she had entered into with several guys on campus. Sex wasn't a part of their relationship: she respected him too much for that. And she just let him think she was a virgin.

But now this.

It was a mile hike into town to the community drug store. Meghan couldn't get there fast enough. She had to run a pregnancy test before David came back to campus from Easter break. Maybe she was worried about nothing. Nonetheless she kept her eyes averted when she paid for her purchase, hurrying as fast as she could back to campus and the privacy of her room.

Quickly collecting her urine, she put the tab into the cup and waited. It didn't take long for her to know that her suspicions were true. What to do?

Abortion was absolutely out of the question. She was still angry that her parents had aborted a child just so her dad could get on with his education and career, robbing her of a sibling she had always wanted. No, she would not even consider abortion. That was final.

Meghan sat down at her desk, took out a yellow tablet, and began to list her options. She wrote:

> 1) Drop out of school and go to one of those houses for single pregnant girls and put the baby up for adoption;
> 2) Face the condemnation on campus, finish the semester, and have a doctor find an adoption for her – maybe a couple who would pay all her expenses;

3) Go home and confess all to her parents, ask for their forgiveness, and hide out there until the baby was born (no, I don't think I can do this one... dad would never forgive me); 4) Tell David what all she had done and hope he would forgive her and help her figure out what to do. 5). . . .

Meghan sat a long time looking out the window of her dorm room. There was no '5' that she could think of. She desperately needed to talk to somebody who could help her think straight. Why hadn't she protected herself? How stupid! And she didn't even know who the father was....

A familiar voice in the hall and a knock on the door and there was Jennie, come back early to study while the campus was quiet. Of course, she could talk to Jennie.

"Hi, Meghan. Want to grab some lunch and catch up on what's happening?" Jennie asked.

They split a hamburger at the Shack Shop while Jennie bubbled about the arrest, the FBI, the Kenya trip. She had so much to tell that she failed to notice how quiet Meghan was. Finally she ran down enough to ask, "So how are things going with you, Meghan?" She was totally unprepared for Meghan's flood of tears.

"Jennie, I'm pregnant." There. It was out. Somehow just saying it made things easier.

"Are you sure? I mean, how could you be? David? You and David?" Jennie reached for the only plausible explanation she could think of, but somehow it didn't seem like David would have sex before marriage.

"I wish it was David. Then I'd maybe know what to do. No, David doesn't know. Nobody knows but you. I just ran the test this morning." Meghan's voice trailed off as she began to sob.

"Now wait," Jennie began. "You ran a home test? Lots of times they give a false positive. Let's not panic. Wait a few days and run another test, then if it's still positive we'll get you to a doctor to check your results. In the meantime, don't tell anyone, especially not David. You've got a good thing going with him and there's no need to mess it up, right?" Jennie put as good a spin on Meghan's situation as she could. She had never asked about the time she found Meghan drunk, what might have caused that to happen. Now it looked like there was a bigger story behind that episode. Looking around at the almost empty Shack, Jennie ventured to ask, "Meghan, what's going on? Is there more you want to tell me?"

Meghan shook her head 'no'. "I'm afraid if I do, you won't be my friend anymore, and I want – I need you to be my friend, Jennie. Maybe I'll talk to the Chaplain, or one of the counselors…. after we get the tests done. Do you think I ought to buy a different kind to be surer of the results?'

Jennie allowed her to have space. "I think that's a good idea. Want to go get it now? It will be a good walk for both of us. And I'll buy it this time. That way if the druggist has any suspicions, she won't know which of us to suspect."

"Thanks, Jennie. It's good to know I can count on you."

The two girls walked nonchalantly out of the Shack. If anyone had been looking, they would have seen two college students just going out for an afternoon walk.

Two days later they ran the second test. It was positive.

A dejected Meghan simply said, "I have to tell David."

## 32.

Riley Singer had to make a return trip to Callegua U to see President Ingram. His boss had been apologetic for asking him to make the long trip again, but Riley didn't mind, hoping he might meet Jennie. She had stayed in his mind since they met. Every girl he met he compared to her and then would decide there just wasn't any comparison: she was his 'it' girl.

Dr. Ben recognized the black car parked in front of the Administration Building. Glancing at his watch, he determined that he had ten minutes before his next class, just enough time to take a stroll through the Ad building. At least he wouldn't be hiding in the bushes!

Ben had kept his distance from Jennie, honoring her wishes in the hopes that she would be less antagonistic toward him. Every day he checked his mail – sometimes twice – waiting for word from Sheriton University. If they hired him, if he had a signed contract, then he could date Jennie because no one could fire him. He was choosing to leave. But now there seemed to be this complication, this handsome stranger....

There was no sign of anyone on the main floor, so Ben bounded up the stairs, two at a time. Again, he saw no one. He was about to go to the third floor where the president's office was when the president and the visitor came down the stairs. Their conversation was obviously very serious.

Ben stepped aside to let them pass, but President Ingram had seen him. "Were you coming up to see me, Ben?" he asked. Then added, "This is Mr. Riley Singer; Mr. Singer, Dr. Adkins of our History Department."

The men exchanged handshakes, then Ben explained that yes, he was on his way to the president's office, but since he was obviously busy, Ben would come by later in the week.

"Are you sure? I could make time for you," responded President Ingram.

"No, no," Ben stammered. "It's nothing that can't be handled later." Then turning to Riley he added, "Nice to meet you and welcome to Callegua U. Enjoy your visit."

"Thanks," replied Riley; and then, "Maybe you can help me. Do you know where I might find a student, Jennie Reyes?"

Ben swallowed hard and was glad he didn't know where she was and could honestly say so.

"Well, thanks anyway," was Riley's answer. "But if you see her on campus, please tell her I need to talk to her. Have her call my cell phone. She has the number." Then turning to the president, said, "Now, where were we?"

Ben took that as his dismissal and headed down the stairs. If he saw Jennie, he would be sure *not* to tell her to call this Singer guy. He could be tough competition and Ben figured it was going to be hard enough to get Jennie to date him, let alone love him.

A last check at the post office produced the fat envelope marked Sheriton University. With trembling hands, Ben carefully opened the flap and pulled out several sheets of paper topped by official Sheriton stationary.

"Dear Dr. Adkins," he read. "We are happy to inform you that you are the unanimous choice of our search committee to join our History Department next fall. You will find the terms of our offer on the following page. If they are satisfactory for you, please fill out the enclosed contract and return it at your earliest convenience." Ben glanced at the rest of the letter, shuffled through the pages, stuffed them back in the envelope, did a little joy jump and then headed out to find Gene and John to tell them the great news.

Meanwhile the mail that would really change his life sat untouched in his mailbox.

Jennie's mail that day also contained a life-changing letter, but she was too busy with Meghan to read it.

### 33.

"Now what?" said Dr. Gene as he scanned the morning's announcements. A special Trustee meeting had been called for early the next week, followed by a special Faculty meeting. Dr. John was hoping for a tenure announcement, and Dr. Ben supposed it was to announce new faculty for the fall.

Rumors flew as the Trustee date drew closer. It was one thing to call a special board meeting, but quite another to follow it immediately with a Faculty meeting. Seats were at a premium in the lecture hall that morning. No one would dare miss this meeting.

President Ingram entered, followed by Riley Singer and two other men dressed in black, plus all the Trustees. Ben was on alert instantly. Whatever was said somehow involved Jennie.

"Members of the Faculty, thank you for coming. Callegua University will need the help of all of you to get through the crisis we face. But first, let me introduce Mr. Riley Singer from the FBI and two of his colleagues from the Attorney General's Office. After I make my presentation, they will answer any questions you may have." The hall was absolutely quiet as the men took their seats behind the podium.

"Some of you have been here long enough to remember a certain football star who played for

Callegua in the 70's. Or you may know his name as
one of our most generous alumni, J.W. Williams,
who as near as the Attorney's Office can discern
from the University's books, has given the college
almost $8.5 million over the past twenty years. Mr.
Williams is under arrest charged with drug
trafficking, which we are told began when he was a
student here. It seems that he is the head of a cartel
that works with South and Central America and
Mexico, Africa, and perhaps worldwide.

The president stopped to take a drink of water
from the glass on the podium, then continued.

"You may be asking yourself what that has to
do with Callegua? To get to the point, the Attorney
General's Office says this is all drug money and the
Justice Department wants the money back."

A collective gasp went across the room. Even
if the college wanted to give it back, not even the
Reserve Fund held that kind of money. Some of the
more conservative faculty immediately blamed the
anti-Christian political atmosphere in Washington.

President Ingram waited until the room was
quiet before adding, "And for Callegua this is not
just about giving back the money. For us it is a
moral issue. Our University does not endorse
illegal acts of any kind and especially does not
approve the buying and selling or use of non-
prescription drugs. Ladies and Gentlemen, we have
a major dilemma: We do not have $8.5 million to
give, but beyond that we will be required to have
representation in court when the Williams case
comes to trial late this year."

No one moved or asked a question for almost
five minutes. What could they do? Insurance
would probably pay for the court defense, but the
$8.5 million was another matter. Yet if they did not
return the money the college would be seen as
accepting and using illicit funds. And what about

the students who were struggling against drugs in a society where almost all their peers had used drugs at one time or another? What kind of example would the University's actions set for them?

Riley Singer had stepped to the podium, ready to receive questions, but the first question was for the president.

One of the Vice Presidents who had been shut out of the Trustee's meeting called out, "Tell us what the Trustees said. What is their reaction? How can they help us?

The president handed the microphone to the Chair of the Trustees. "You can imagine what a shock this is to all of us," he began. "We have known and worked with Mr. Williams for many years, always under honorable circumstances. We had great difficulty believing what these gentlemen from the FBI told us, but they have informed us in great detail. We obviously were taken in by the man, as, unfortunately were his daughter, wife, and son, the latter two of whom went with our interim group to Kenya."

"But you asked what we decided. Nothing, except for establishing the clear concept that we must return the money. We did raise the idea of a major fund drive and between us around the table we raised $1 million to start. But we need your approval and enthusiastic support to carry out such a fund drive when we have just finished raising $5 million for new dormitories. But ladies and gentlemen, the last thing Callegua needs is a scandal with her name tied up with drugs. We are asking your cooperation to keep this whole thing as quiet as possible."

"Fat chance of that!" whispered Dr. Gene. "Ben, you are one lucky guy to be getting out of here. The rest of us are probably stuck for life. What university would want to hire faculty who worked for such a simpleton school as to accept money without questioning its source. You know, anything goes to keep the doors open." His look of disgust said it all.

Now that the Trustee Chair had sat down, the questions began to pour out toward Riley. "If the school pays back the money, do we have to go to court?" "Can the trial go on without naming Callegua?" "Would the courts award us the money because we accepted it in good faith?" "What about the time period over which Williams gave us the money?" "Are some of his gifts too old to be considered?"

And so it went for the next hour until all who had a question, had asked it. Ben was still puzzled. What connection did Jennie have with all of this? She certainly didn't know Williams, and even if his son and wife had gone to Kenya with the team, that was only a casual acquaintance. Something must have happened in Jennie's presence that pulled her into this, and he intended to find out what it was.

The meeting adjourned, but small clusters of faculty remained to talk, some to each other, some to the Trustee Chair and President Ingram, and one or two to the FBI men. Even though it put a sour taste in his mouth, Ben approached Riley Singer, reminded him of their previous meeting in the Ad Building, and asked, "If you can tell me, what does all this have to do with Jennie Reyes? She's one of our top students and I'd hate for anything to smear her name, and for that matter, her application to med school."

Riley sized up the professor standing before him. Nice looking guy, probably about 24, no wedding ring, maybe looking for a wife. Maybe he was his competition for Jennie.

"I can only tell you that she witnessed a transaction at the airport, worked with the son to arrange the trip and was in Kenya with him. We'll want her for a witness, especially if he turns out to be in the drug business with his father."

Riley's response was sobering for Ben. A trial could mess up Jennie's grades this semester, and they were crucial to her med school applications. He asked, "And when do you expect this might go to trial?"

"Probably not before summer. Of course the way the courts work these days it could run into a year or two, what with appeals and all."

Relieved, Ben thanked Riley and left to find Jennie. Maybe the faculty was supposed to keep the Williams money case hush-hush, but Jennie needed to know as much as he could supply, in order to protect herself. Besides it would give him a legitimate reason to talk to her.

Jennie, meanwhile, had read her mail and knew she had to talk to Ben, and because of the arrangements they needed to make, the sooner they talked, the better.

### 34.

Sue opened her email to find the message from Trisha:

"Sue, when you left here, I had no idea I would need your help so soon. While we were at the airport seeing off the group, rebels came and burned down two of our buildings, one with all our supplies in it. No one was hurt, but does your offer of money still hold? Whatever you can give us would be a blessing from God. We all send our love and gratitude to you. Trisha"

Tears streamed down Sue's cheeks as she thought of the children and workers in the orphanage, so cruelly treated. She was thankful everyone was safe, and then she realized just how important it was for her to know quickly what the FBI expected of her. Doug had gone home, and she knew she had to act on her own.

Almost as if someone had read her mind, the phone rang. It was Riley Singer, the last agent she had talked to."Mrs. Williams? Riley Singer here. Would it be all right if I came by this morning? I think I have some good news for you."

"Good news? I could use some of that! But you know I'll have to have my lawyer here, so I'll see if she can join us and then get back to you." Their goodbyes were said and Sue called the lawyer's office.

"You are in luck, Sue," responded the receptionist. "Believe it or not, you are on her calendar for this morning. Apparently she was going to ask you to come in after she talked to Agent Singer yesterday afternoon, so yes, she will come to your home at 10."

"That was almost too easy," thought Sue, "I wonder what's going to happen now?"

Promptly at 10 a.m. the agent and the lawyer arrived, met each other on the front porch, and shook hands as if in agreement about something. A few minutes later the three were sitting at the dining room table with papers spread from one end of the table to the other. Sue listened in amazement as Agent Singer explained the numbers, testimonies, and other papers, including the bill of sale they had found in J.W.'s files. Finally he summed up the purpose of his visit.

"So you see, Mrs. Williams, we are absolutely sure that you are an innocent victim in this case, as are your son and daughter. It is only your husband that we will take to trial. When that time comes, we will call the three of you as witnesses, but in the meantime, you are no longer under surveillance. Further, the Attorney General's Office has determined that the bank accounts in your name were not acquired with drug money, so you are free to use those funds. The house, however, was paid for by Mr. Williams, and it must be sold and the money returned to the Justice Department. Using your own funds, you are welcome to purchase it from them if you choose for today's market price, which we will work with you to determine. Your clothes have little or no market value, so you may keep them. Likewise, anything owned by your children will not be confiscated."

Immediately Sue's thoughts were with Trisha. There was money for the orphanage, and she was free to use it! The house? She didn't want the house with all its memories of J.W.'s lying ways. Yes, she would sell the house and – suddenly her head and heart felt like they would explode -- she would sell the house and furniture, give away all her clothes and go live and work at the orphanage in Kenya. Yes, she would. She would give the mission her money…. and herself!

To Agent Singer she merely smiled and thanked him for his conscientious work, and then added, "But I won't be needing the house nor any of its furnishings because I have decided to live and work in Kenya at the orphanage. Am I free to travel there soon?" Sue's heart was pounding. She felt like she was on an adrenaline high.

"Ordinarily I would say no, not until the trial is over, but that could be two years from now, so I'll check with the department. I think they will trust you to return when we need you to witness. I'll give you a call this afternoon. And now if you'll excuse me, I need to answer a call from the office. These papers are all copies, so you may keep them, or maybe let your lawyer keep them for you." Riley shook hands with the two women and minutes later drove away.

The lawyer stayed with Sue, drawing up a trust fund of two million dollars for the Kenya orphanage with Trisha and the governing board as trustees, and then completing divorce papers. Sue no longer wanted to be Sue Williams, so she legally took back her maiden name and became Sue Pendella.

When the lawyer had left and Sue was alone, she sat down at her computer and sent emails to Doug and Laina and Trisha, telling them what she had done, and assuring Doug and Laina that there was still $500,000 left for them to divide when she was gone. Then she added the news that the house would be sold to satisfy the Justice Department's claim, and she would shortly be returning to Kenya to live and work there with Trisha, so that if they wanted anything from the house, they must take it ASAP.

To Laina she separately said she would be sending her grandmother's jewelry, and to Doug, she gave her two Jaguars. She welcomed their questions but informed them her mind was made up. Kenya was where she believed God wanted her to be.

Trisha responded joyfully to Sue's email. She had long wanted a partner to help her lead the mission and now Sue, so new a Christian and her newly bonded friend, was coming to help her.

Next Sue called a real estate agent and listed the house for sale. Then she contacted an estate agent to schedule the sale of all the furnishings, including original paintings, valuable antiques – anything of value. The money earned would all go to Justice, so she called Agent Singer and told him his property was now on the market and she would

stay in touch.  He in turn told her she was free to go
to Kenya.

Not forgetting Trisha's email of the morning,
she had her bank transfer $10,000 to the mission
account so they could begin to rebuild what had
been burned.  And finally, she went online to order
dozens of layettes, children's shoes, boys' shirts and
girls' skirts, bedding, towels and wash cloths,
dishtowels, body soap, dish soap, food....
everything she could remember from her stay at the
orphanage that might be needed now that their
supply building was gone.

Sue was exhausted by nightfall, but finished
the day by sending Trisha an email telling her what
all she could expect to arrive, giving her the news
about the new money in her account, and promising
to come very soon…as soon as the house and
furnishings were sold.

It took her a long time to go to sleep that
night.  In one day she had changed her whole life,
but she felt no fear, only exhilaration.  She guessed
she had J.W. to thank for pushing her into a new
life.  And God.  Surely that heart-pounding moment
when she knew she would go to Kenya to help
Trisha was God speaking to her, for she had felt
totally at peace ever since.  Doug and Laina would
never understand her giving her money to the
orphanage instead of to them, nor would they
understand what she was about to do, but that was
all right.  They were adults now, making their own
living, and they would have enough when she
passed away.

Lying in bed, Sue reviewed every detail of the
day.  When she finished, she turned her eyes upward
and whispered, "Dear God, if I have held back
anything, please show it to me because, God, I have
decided to surrender all to you, even my life."  With
that final prayer, she was swiftly asleep, at peace

deep in her soul that what she had done was exactly right.

## 35.

When David Belkin came back to campus after Easter Break, he was eager to see Meghan. Over the holiday he had decided that Meghan was the girl he wanted in his life. He loved her. He loved her long blond hair and the way she flicked it aside when it chanced to fall over her face. He loved her musical laugh and fun-filled spirit, her spirit of adventure. He loved the way she fit under his arm just right and the warm, feminine smell about her.

There was one big thing that they hadn't discussed, however, and he knew he couldn't commit to Meghan until she told him how she felt about being the wife of a minister who would be on call 24/7, not always there for her or the family if they had one, often gone to meetings leaving her with long, lonely evenings. Was she up to that? Would she take on that kind of life, because for him there was no turning away from his calling?

Another reason he wanted to see Meghan right away was because time was running out. He would graduate in two months and then move on to Princeton University for Seminary studies, so they would be separating. Unless…. he dared to think how they would make it, but maybe she would marry him this summer and go with him, maybe work to help with their living expenses. That was a lot to ask when Meghan was just finishing her freshman year.

All these thoughts were running through David's head as he entered the girl's dorm and rang Meghan's call bell. He felt eager, anxious,

impatient even, while he waited for her. When she
did not appear, he realized that she might not have
come back to campus yet, and he turned to leave.

"David?" Meghan's voice was hoarse from
crying. "I'm here."

"Meghan? What's wrong?" Her eyes were
red and puffy like she had been crying a long time.
Her hair looked unwashed, her clothes disheveled as
though they had been slept in.

"Oh, David, there is something I must tell
you, but if I do you will probably never speak to me
again." Meghan began to cry, her shoulders
shaking in agony as if she could shake off the words
she must say.

"Don't cry, Meghan. Nothing can be as bad
as that," was David's response. He put his arm
around her shoulders and guided her out of the
building. "Let's go find a bench and you can tell me
all about it."

His touch made her cry harder. David was
such a good person and she was in love with him,
but she knew he could never be hers, not now, not
with her carrying a baby, a baby that wasn't even
his. She followed him obediently to a secluded
bench where they sat, his arm around her and her
head on his shoulder, until Meghan's tears finally
ceased.

She had practiced for this difficult, dreaded
moment. "David, I'm so sorry. You will think I am
terrible, and I guess I am." She paused, looked at
the ground so she wouldn't see his eyes, then said
simply, "I'm pregnant."

David withdrew his arm from her shoulders
and instead turned her toward him, tipping up her
chin so he could look into her eyes. "You're what?"
was his hollow reply.

"I'm pregnant," repeated Meghan, wishing

she couldn't see the anguish on David's face.

"But how? I mean, who?" And then, "I thought you were a virgin. I…I don't know what to say." David backed away from her, then overwhelmed by what she had just told him, doubled over, arms crossed over his stomach, and began to moan, "Oh God, oh God, oh God."

Meghan laid her hand on his shoulder, trying to comfort him. "David, it was just before we started dating. I just hooked up with a guy one afternoon. I don't even know his name. I never dreamed this would happen, but I was careless…"

"Careless? What are you telling me, Meghan, that this was something you did all the time? Just hook up with somebody? How many somebodies?" David was angry now. Meghan had deceived him. He stood up and turned to face her. "I don't know you at all! And to think I wanted to marry you! What are you, the campus whore?"

The minute he said it, he wanted to take it back. After all, this was Meghan who just minutes ago he was in love with. He had condemned her instead of listening, finding out what was the cause of her behavior. Some minister he'd make! How many people in his future would pour out their distress to him, and find him cold, heartless? He fell to his knees. "Oh Meghan, I'm sorry. I didn't mean those words. Please, please forgive me."

Meghan took his hands in hers and said, "It's all right, David. I deserve it. If you're willing to listen, I'll tell you what has happened to me since last Thanksgiving. I should have told you when we began to get serious about one another, but I just couldn't. I didn't want to lose you, and I thought maybe you never had to know…." Her voice trailed off.

A breeze had come up and the sun was beginning to disappear over the horizon.

"Meghan, I want you to tell me your story, but not now, not yet," began David. "Look, it's getting cool, we both need to eat, and I think we both need to separate for the night so we can think this thing through. Then I'll take you off campus for lunch tomorrow. I think that will give me enough time to be ready to listen. Let's walk back to the dorm, ok?" He took Meghan's hand and pulled her to her feet. Together they walked, not touching, until at the dorm's front door David turned away with, "See you tomorrow. G'night."

It was a toss and turn night for each of them. At 7:00 a.m. Meghan's phone rang.

"Meghan, I don't want to wait. Let's go have breakfast. Can you be ready in ten minutes?"

Meghan looked in the mirror; maybe if she pulled her hair back into a ponytail, she could do that? Into the phone she said, "Sure, David. I'll be in front of the dorm." And in ten minutes she was.

It was to that same diner in the woods where Drs. Ben, John, and Gene went for privacy from campus eyes that a composed David took Meghan for breakfast. The diner was almost empty, but they nonetheless chose a booth at the very back where no one would see them. Food was not on their minds, however, and they scarcely noticed what they were eating.

"Ok, Meghan, I want to know you, so I think you should go back before whatever happened at Thanksgiving. Tell me everything. I promise I won't get angry or call you names." David had spent most of the night praying that whatever Meghan told him he would be able to accept, no matter how terrible it was, although he couldn't imagine Meghan, his lovely Meghan could have done much wrong.

Meghan began with what a wonderful home she grew up in, with devoted parents to each other and her, until she came to Callegua, met Jennie, and discovered that when her parents were in college and before they were married, they had aborted a baby. She told him how she had confronted them and discovered also that she was an in vitro baby and was carried by a surrogate mother because her own mother had so much scar tissue from the abortion.

"I exploded with anger," she said, "because I felt they had lied to me all those years, were the worst kind of hypocrites, pretending to be so Christian in their church and community. You know, David, how I feel about abortion, that it is taking a life. And they not only did that, but they robbed me of the brother or sister I could have had." Her voice rose with unresolved anger and David had to remind her to speak quietly lest others hear.

"So," Meghan went on, "I decided I would make them pay for what they had done to me. I came back to school, and the guy who drove me back didn't want any money, but he did want sex, so I....." Meghan hesitated. She hated to tell this part, but everything had to be said if David would ever forgive her. Even if they broke up, she thought, which would probably happen, it somehow felt good to tell someone what had happened.

"I took him up on it. Then he gave me a bottle of Vodka to take back to my room, and since I had never tasted alcohol, I had a couple of Dixie cups of the stuff. Then I saw the guy the next day at the Shack and asked him if he wanted more sex. He said sure, so we did it again."

David was pinned to his seat. This could happen at Callegua? To Meghan? Of course, the campus had been fairly empty because of Thanksgiving break...

Meghan went on to tell him how she had drunk all the Vodka, been really sick from it, how

Jennie had rescued her so no one would know..."
And then I found out that I really wanted more sex.
Not alcohol; never again for that. But I had
awakened my body, so whenever I had a chance, I
took it, which is why I don't know who the father of
this baby is."

David waited while Meghan drank her coffee,
waited for whatever else was part of her story.
Finally he asked, "But Meghan, you never pressed
me for sex. We've been dating two months now,
and you have been almost chaste. Why, if you had
such a need?"

"Because I respect you, David. And I wanted
you to think the best of me. I liked you and now
I've fallen in love with you. I thought perhaps we
would marry, but of course that is out of the
question now." A tear rolled down Meghan's cheek.

They both were quiet for a few minutes. Then
David reached across the table and took Meghan's
hand.

"I still love you, Meghan. I don't know what
we will do about the baby, but I still love you and
want to marry you, if you'll have me."

"But David, a minister can't have a wife like
me. If anyone ever found out that I had a child
without being married, your congregations might
reject us both. The church might not even ordain
you!" Meghan did not want to ruin David's life.
She would have to break off their relationship.

"We'll cross that bridge when we come to it,
Meghan. I have heard the worst and I forgive you
and accept you. I want you to make peace with
your parents. That's most important. In a few days
we'll figure out what to do, but you, Meghan, some
day will be my wife, no matter what. I love you
now and I always will.

As soon as they were back in the car David
took Meghan in his arms and kissed her thoroughly.

Christ's words that he had read over and over last night he had put into practice: "Forgive even seventy times seven..." and "Love one another, even as I have loved you." This was the beginning of a lifetime of practicing those words.

When they slid apart into their separate seats, David said, "Meghan, I think I know what to do. The semester is almost over; I will graduate, so let's get married now, in the college chapel. Jennie and Samuel can stand up with us. Everyone will think the baby is mine anyway, so let's make it mine. From now on I'm the father of the baby you're carrying. It will be born this summer after school is out, and no one need be the wiser. What do you say? Shall we get married, say, next week?

Before Meghan could answer, he added, "Classes start up again tomorrow, so let's go into the city today and get a license, and we can go to emergency at the hospital and get our blood tests. I'm sure they'll do it or send us someplace where we can get the tests done. Then we can have the Chaplain perform the ceremony. Ok, Meghan? You want to get married? After all, we're going to have a baby!"

And so it was that in the very hospital that Meghan's mother had an abortion twenty years before, Meghan had a blood test so she and David could marry and give parents and a loving welcome to the baby growing within her.

The following Wednesday, one month after Meghan's 18th birthday, the campus Chaplain married David and Meghan in a short ceremony. The bride and groom wore jeans and Callegua U sweatshirts, and Jennie and Samuel were their witnesses. Jennie took some pictures and then the four of them went to the Shack Shop to celebrate.

Mr. and Mrs. David Belkin had launched themselves into married life with a baby on the way.

131

## 36.

Laina could not believe the email. Never in her strangest dreams would she believe that her mother would give her money to an African mission, and then go there to live and work. She got Doug on the phone.

"Yeah, sis. Mom had a "conversion" experience on the trip, so when she was faced with giving up everything Dad had paid for, which included the house and all the furniture, I guess she just lost it. She could have bought the house back from the Justice Department, but seems like she didn't want to live there anymore. And I would have bought it, but it was sold by the time I found out it was for sale. Weird, huh?" Doug had been just as floored as Laina at Sue's actions. "I understand they also want the $8.5 million he gave to Callegua. Not surprised, though, that she didn't give her money to the school, after all you've told me about her freshman year."

"Meantime we have only what we earn with no help from her, right?" Laina's income was enough, but not great.

"That's about it," replied Doug. Then with concern for his sister who was just starting her career, "Will you be ok?"

Meanwhile the object of their conversation was on her way to Kenya, in flight as they spoke. Sue's house had sold quickly, she hired people to run the estate sale, and within days of the sale she had settled with Justice. Next she had taken her designer clothes to a commission shop and directed them to send any money from the sale to Laina. Her mother's jewelry had been sent to Laina as well, but her own jewelry she decided to keep in a safety deposit box in the event that someday she might want to give it to a grandchild. She sent the key to Doug in case he needed it. So, when everything was in order, she called Agent Singer and told him she would be leaving the next week for Kenya, gave him Trisha's email so he could contact her, and bought her air ticket. In her one suitcase were thrift store clothes, which was all she would need at the mission.

Trisha was at the airport waiting for her, with the news that Samuel would be arriving right after his graduation, and the children and workers were planning a big party to welcome both of them. They chatted like schoolgirls as the Land Rover, with Trisha at the wheel, bumped along.

It took about three days for Sue to catch up with the new time zone and rest from her travel. Wherever she went on the mission grounds the children followed her, each wanting her attention, and she loved it. Soon she was assisting Trisha with teaching, helping with meals for the children, filling in wherever she was needed.

Several weeks passed. Sue was content. She was loved, accepted, and daily her Christian life was nourished by prayer times and conversations with all the adults on the mission, especially Trisha. Every day she would sit with her Bible and read. It was new to her, and fascinating. She wondered why she had missed this when she was growing up.

But then she would remember the lifestyle of those early years, her rebellion against her parents, the drugs, the weird parties, all the alcohol she drank. And of course, J.W. Occasionally she would have to sweep her mind clean of the night at Callegua when she was gang raped while J.W. encouraged the guys. And yet she had married him! Even after he put all the blame on her for stealing the tests that horrible afternoon when she had to face the Student Council and was told to leave

Callegua. Only now did she realize what the other students must have thought of her....

But God had forgiven all that, had just been waiting for her to ask for forgiveness. And then in this blessed place she had found Him again.

She had just finished reading and praying one afternoon when there was a commotion in the yard in front of the activity building. Five tall dark men were yelling at Peter and Trisha. The other workers had gathered around but stayed back from the men. Sue hurried to join Trisha.

"You want us to spare this mission? This Christian mission? Infidels! You do not worship Allah! You are our enemies!" The leader spat on the ground.

"But these children are innocent. They are the future of our country," Peter was saying as Sue walked up. "What do we have that we can give you so you will leave us alone?" He was not afraid except for the children.

It was then Sue saw the guns they carried.

"Money. Lots of money. We know you have it. You buy lots of food. We need food and weapons. One thousand dollars we need today, or we will burn your buildings."

"That is all we have, but we will give it to you in exchange for our safety."

Peter looked at Trisha, who nodded 'yes'. They could give the rebels money today and then figure out what to do later. He called one of his helpers who knew where the cash was kept, and while he was getting it, Peter kept talking to the men, trying to reason with them, telling them the mission was a good thing for Kenya and they needed to protect it, not burn it. They laughed and spit at him, calling him stupid for taking care of worthless children who had no parents.

"If it weren't for the money, old man," said the leader, "I would line them up and kill them all right now." He eagerly grabbed the money when the worker returned, started to leave with his men, then turned back. "One more thing. My men need a woman. How about this little white woman?" He grabbed Trisha by the arm. "She would suit them just fine."

"We made a deal for money, not a woman," exclaimed Peter. "Let her go. She is nothing to you, but our children need her. She is their mother."

The men had turned around and come back to their leader. They began to circle around Trisha, poke her with their guns, pat her body with knowing glances to each other. "She'd do fine. We love white women," said one of them.

"No! Let her go," said Peter, trying hard to keep control of his anger. He knew that if he struck the leader, which was what he wanted to do, all would be lost. Silently he prayed for help.

Sue stepped forward. Trisha didn't deserve this, not after a lifetime of work building the mission, saving these children's lives.

"Let her go," Sue said. "You can take me."

"No, Sue, no," Trisha and Peter exclaimed together. "They will rape you and leave you to die! You can't do this!"

"What other choice do we have?" Sue spoke calmly. Her life was not important any more. All her life was in order back in the States. Doug and Laina were raised, on their own. And God would protect her, or claim her if she died.

"I will go with you," she said to the leader, "but only if you agree to leave this mission alone. If I have to buy it with my life, I will."

The leader let go of Trisha, grabbed Sue and tossed her to his men, who went running from the compound, dragging her behind them, with the leader fast on their heels.

Peter and Trisha watched, stunned speechless. Suddenly Trisha was aware of all the workers and her job to take charge. "Let's go inside. There's nothing we can do."

Three days later they found Sue's mutilated body in the tall grass not far from the mission. She had given her life for them.

## 37.

The news of Sue's death was noted in the campus newspaper and the Kenya team held a memorial service in the college chapel, so recently the site of David and Meghan's marriage. Both Samuel and Jennie spoke about her spiritual transformation. All of them were glad that Sue had found her conversion experience while they were in Kenya, and they thanked God for her choice to use her life to save the orphanage. Privately most of the students wondered if they would have been so courageous.

It was Doug Williams' email that had given the news to Jennie. He also told her that Sue had left two million dollars in trust for the orphanage to ensure its financial future. What the email did not say was that he and Laina had settled everything with the FBI, and still each of them inherited over a quarter of a million dollars from their mother.

In the President's office the news of Sue's death immediately set off a flurry of activity and the Trustees and the University's lawyers tried to find out if this would have any effect on the $8.5 million the Justice Department expected from the school as payback for the money J.W. had given them over the last twenty years. The $5 million ex-President

Clayton had raised was already committed to the
new science building under construction and it
would take another two million to finish it.

Graduation was eminent. If nothing changed,
the Trustees intended to ask the alumni to make
substantial contributions to both efforts: the
building fund and the reimbursement of the drug
money. Fortunately, they had never had to use their
liability insurance, and it would pay five million
toward the FBI payment. The lawyers were in
discussion with the Department to accept the
insurance money as full payment, but until J.W.'s
trial, no agreement could be made.

The trial was inching its way through the legal
system. It would be at least a year before the case
came to court, maybe two years. The Trustees and
faculty had committed themselves to a million and a
half, but this was being kept very quiet. Meantime,
there was nothing the administration could do but
try to raise at least two million, and if the Justice
Department took it, raise another two million for the
science building.

Dr. John and Dr. Gene had agreed to serve on
the faculty fund-raising committee, which left them
little time for Dr. Ben, so they didn't know that he
and Jennie would be attending a history conference
in New York City, starting two days after
graduation.

### 38.

It had taken a couple of weeks before Ben had
dug down through the papers on his desk to find the
invitation to accompany Jennie to the National
Convention of Historians in New York as the
winner of the scholarship toward her graduate work.

Ben was beside himself when he read the
letter. Four days with Jennie! Four days when he

was no longer a professor at Callegua. And there was no way she could turn him down.

Jennie had received an invitation also, noting that the professor who had nominted her should accompany her. She was happy to have an all-expense-paid trip to New York City, but not happy that she would have to go with Dr. Adkins. Nonetheless, that was the price she would have to pay.

To prepare for the trip the two had met several times to sketch out possible speeches, set up travel arrangements, and, as it turned out, to get better acquainted. Since Dr. Ben was leaving Callegua to move east to Sheriton U, he felt perfectly at ease to talk to Jennie whenever he saw her on campus. Twice he took her off-campus for dinner, but he kept his conversation strictly business-like.

The second dinner happened just after the news of Sue's death. Jennie was sad and found herself unexpectedly teary-eyed.

"Why don't you tell me about your time together in Kenya?" asked Ben when they had finished their meal. "I'd like to know what kind of person Sue was." He hoped he was as disarming as he wanted to be.

Jennie was caught off guard by this caring side of Dr. Ben. Maybe he wasn't so bad after all. "Well, Sue was my mother's roommate at Callegua twenty some years ago," she began, "and my mom told me a lot of things that happened to her and Sue before I came here as a freshman. Much of it was pretty unbelievable and it made me very curious about Sue. I guess I expected to meet somebody who had spent her life strung out on drugs."

"Then why did you let her go as a chaperone for the Kenya group? Wasn't that a little chancy?" Ben remembered her turning him down, but they took a woman that might have been on drugs?

"Not really. Doug, her son, gave her a good recommendation, and he was going on the trip too, so I figured if there was a problem, he would take care of it." Jennie remembered that she had said ok to Sue in order to keep Dr. Ben from going so she could keep him away from herself. She quickly continued with the story of Sue in Kenya in order to avoid the obvious question of why she had chosen Sue over Dr. Ben.

"She turned out to be a gracious, cultured woman, and I think she was as anxious to meet me as I was to meet her. At the orphanage she worked hard, helped cook, took care of the more difficult children, and taught some of the women to make their own clothes. She cut up the designer clothes she had brought for fabric. At first she hung back, but about mid-month she changed, became outgoing, so helpful, as I said. Then on the bus to the airport she told the group that she had been converted, had a Christ experience during the month. I think the Sue that died was vastly different from the Sue who went to Kenya. To think she voluntarily gave herself in place of Trisha! And left the orphanage almost everything she had." Jennie's voice trailed off as she thought about Sue's death.

Ben reached across the table and covered Jennie's hand with his own. "Jennie, I'm so sorry that the trip had to be scarred in this way," he said.

She pulled back her hand. "Scarred? Are you kidding? Her death made the whole trip worthwhile, to see the transformation that Christ can make in a life will always stay with me. And the money she left the orphanage will allow it to go for many years, as long as Trisha feels there is a need!"

Again Ben realized what a special person Jennie was. Her creamy complexion and long, flowing black hair and flashing dark eyes, the beauty that she was, all that attracted him to her in the first place, was the least part of her. If it was possible he was falling ever more in love with her—with her mind, her spirit, her innate strength. He had to win her; he had to marry her! Whatever it took, he couldn't let Jennie get away from him.

At last they turned to the final details for the New York trip: what hotel they would stay in, what their responsibilities would be at the convention, and what sightseeing they might be able to work into their schedule. Jennie had resigned herself to being in his company most of the four days, and in fact liked the idea of being with a man in New York. It made her feel safe. *He* made her feel safe, which was a surprise to her.

Because they were leaving for New York from campus, she stayed after the semester ended for graduation, so she got to see an excited Samuel receive his diploma and wave goodbye to the class. A car was waiting to take him to the airport to fly back home to Kenya and his family. Watching him, Jennie realized that she, too, was excited about going to the airport in two days, even if it meant being with Dr. Ben for four whole days. Not long ago, that would have been a high price to pay to gain her scholarship, but now? She resolved to enjoy herself, no matter what....

## 39.

"Mom?"

Angie braced herself for what Meghan might say next. There had been so many angry phone calls and she and Ron knew that graduation was over, yet Meghan had not come home. It was with apprehension and relief that she heard Meghan's voice.

"Meghan! We're so glad to hear from you. Where are you? Why haven't you come home? "

Ron walked in the door so Angie switched on the speakerphone so he could hear the conversation.

"That's why I'm calling. I'm with someone I want you to meet, and we're on the road now. We just stopped to eat, so we should be there in about an hour. Is Dad home?" Meghan turned to wink at David. She was really going to surprise her parents this time.

"He just walked in, so I'll try to have him stay until you get here. He has appointments this afternoon with new clients. Very important, but he heard you on speakerphone and is nodding his head yes, so I guess we'll both be here."

Angie was afraid to ask anything about the friend Meghan was bringing lest it set off an angry tangent. She had learned to just listen and agree, so after Meghan's "okay, in about an hour…," Angie quietly hung up the phone, looked at Ron and said, "What now?"

When David and Meghan got out of the car, Ron was waiting for them on the front porch. One look at Meghan and he summed up the situation immediately: their daughter was definitely pregnant, and this guy was the one who was responsible. He could feel the anger rise up inside, so that when Meghan tried to hug him, he pushed her away. What else was she going to do to them? How much more could she hurt Angie?

"Dad, I want you to meet my husband, David Belkin."

David's extended hand went untouched as Ron reeled under "husband." Is that what Meghan said? Husband? She was married? Without telling them? When? Where did it happen? Suddenly he regretted ever sending Meghan to college.

"Dad," Meghan said, "Shake hands with David. He's going to be part of our family for a lifetime." She paused, then added, "And how about a hug for your daughter?"

Ron was in shock again. His daughter wanted a hug, after all the hatred she had spewed on them? She wanted a hug?

Meghan didn't wait for him to respond but threw her arms around her father, and with tears running down her cheeks whispered, "Dad, I'm so sorry…so sorry I've hurt you so. Please forgive me…."

Angie looked on in amazement from the front room window. She couldn't bring herself to go outside. It was clear that Meghan was pregnant, just like she had been in her freshman year. What would she say to her daughter? And the young man…. he looked like such a nice fellow, so clean cut. He could almost be a young Ron….

Then they were through the door and in the living room, Ron and Meghan with their arms around each other and the young man standing behind, looking slightly embarrassed.

"Angie," Ron stammered, "meet our new daughter and her husband David." He had begun to recover from the shock, now stepping backward so Meghan and David stood together in front of Angie.

At the sight of her mother, Meghan began to sob. She loved her mother and father, but she knew now what her mother had gone through in college, why she, no, they decided to have an abortion, and how they must have struggled with their decision all through their marriage. And she knew they loved her without question, even when she had been so ugly to them this year. She had even crushed her parents' dreams of her wedding, of her dad walking her down the aisle of their church. They were not

bad, hypocritical people. They were deep
Christians who had practiced forgiveness and love
for her, no matter what she did. Now, one more
time, she was expecting them to simply forgive and
forget, accept their only daughter's marriage, and be
joyous over being grandparents. That was a lot to
expect.

It was more than Angie could give. Perhaps
after she had heard their story her emotions would
catch up with her mind, but for now she sternly
invited them into the kitchen for a cup of tea, then
turned without touching Meghan and led the way.

Meghan's plaintive, tear filled voice followed
her: "Mother, I did terrible things to you and Dad
and I'm so sorry. Please forgive me. I did awful
things to myself as well, and to David who loves
me, even enough to be the father of my baby, when
he doesn't have to be." Meghan paused for her
mother's response, but Angie just kept walking
toward the kitchen. "Please, mother, please…."
Her voice trailed off. What else could she say to
break her mother's silence?

Angie motioned for them to sit around the
table while she reached into the refrigerator for left
over pie. She had already made a pot of coffee after
Meghan's phone call, and now the simple task of
serving pie helped her through the surge of thoughts
rolling within her. Meghan wanted forgiveness for
all the angry words and actions of the past few
months; somehow she was married; and she was
pregnant, but if Angie understood correctly, her
husband was not the father. What on earth had
Meghan been doing?

Aloud she said, "Meghan, I think you have a
lot to tell us before we decide to forgive you. It's
just not that easy." Then turning to David, she
added, "I'm sorry, David, that our daughter has

dragged you into the mess she apparently has made of her life."

"Excuse me, Mrs. Kronen, but it's not like that. I love Meghan and asked her to marry me before I knew what had happened to her, but it didn't make any difference to me. I loved her then and I love her now. She's going to make a great mother, and hopefully a great minister's wife."

Now it was Ron's turn. "Son, you don't know what you're saying. A minister's wife? Meghan? Angry, hate-filled Meghan? You are either stupid or love has warped your mind."

Meghan began to cry again. "Please, all of you, try to be calm and listen to what happened to me at college," she said, wiping her tears and getting control of herself. "Then maybe we can talk reasonably."

And so they sat around the kitchen table and heard Meghan's story. Sometimes tears flowed, or the parents squeezed each other's hands, or they stared at the floor. In the few minutes it took, Ron and Angie relived their past, wept for their daughter, struggled with how she had become pregnant, and were amazed by David's acceptance, even to risking his future ministry by marrying Meghan.

When Meghan finished, they sat in silence.

At last Ron spoke. "David, Meghan, your mother and I want to congratulate you on your love and marriage. Welcome, David, into our little family. You will be the son we never were able to have." Then, looking straight into Meghan's eyes he said, "And Meghan, you are our dearest love. We are sorry that you had to go through so much to discover love again, and that you thought we didn't love you, but of course we never stopped loving you, never stopped praying for you. We give your marriage our blessing and the baby that is even now at the table with us."

Then, breaking the seriousness of the moment, he said, "But we're not sure we're old enough to be grandparents!"

Laughter spilled across the table. Angie got up and hugged her daughter, her young husband, and Ron. Soon the kitchen was filled with hugs all around, more tears, and the pie that minutes before no one could eat became celebration food.

Angie thought it was the best pie she ever made.

Ron never made it to his appointments.

## 40.

The Historical Society had insisted that Jennie and Ben travel First Class to and from New York. Jennie was amazed at the difference from the economy flight she was on going to Kenya. The meals were superb: breakfast and lunch were cooked in the flight deck kitchen. Had she wanted alcohol, she could have had it simply by asking, and the headsets were free for the in-flight movie. She wasn't used to such luxury.

She had dressed up for the trip, rather than traveling in the jeans she had worn to Kenya. The weather was warming up, so she had packed lightweight tops, an extra pair of slacks, an unlined jacket that she could wear with everything, and a smart cocktail dress for the formal dinner and presentation.

Her mother had sent her a shoulder wrap and her sparkling necklace that Jennie had worn when she played 'dress-up' when she was a little girl. Joan had also sent a pair of dangling earrings set with tiny crystal stones that would catch the light. Jennie was grateful to her mother for these gifts.

She might be going to a history convention, but she certainly didn't want to look like a nerd.

Ben was in sophisticated, professorial, casual clothes, but he might as well have been wearing rags for all Jennie noticed. He was sitting beside her, of course, but as soon as she could she put on her headphones and locked into the movie, making conversation impossible. She might have to travel with him, but she would preserve their separateness.

When the movie finished, Jennie covered herself with a blanket, put the white pillow behind her head, and feigned sleep for most of the rest of the flight.

Ben was not put off by Jennie's behavior. In fact, he saw it as a challenge. He had four days in New York. Lots of things could happen in that time, but now, sitting this close to the girl he wanted to marry, he would read a magazine, bide his time, and not intrude into her space.

"Smooth landing, wasn't it?" Ben asked Jennie after the pilot had set the plane down at JFK. "I always feel better when I'm back on the ground." He pulled their bags down from the overhead compartment, then added, "Let's go."

Since First Class deplaned as soon as the doors were open, the two quickly found themselves in a sea of people going every which way in the terminal. Everyone seemed to be in a great hurry. It took effort for the two of them to stay together while they made their way to the hotel desk where they were to meet their host.

Over the heads of the crowd Jennie spied a sign that read "REYES". The gentleman holding it looked exactly like she expected an official of the Historical Society to look: short, hair combed over to hide his bald spot, dark suit and tie, slightly rumpled white shirt, and scuffed black shoes.

"Dr. Singleton," was his two-word introduction, hand extended. His wide smile upon meeting Jennie was accented by his hand on the middle of her back, steering her through the crowd toward the waiting taxi, leaving Ben to follow. He was clearly delighted that such a beautiful young woman was the honoree. Remembering the task he had been assigned by the committee to attend to her every need, he savored the next three days.

Jennie had never been in such traffic. New York's great, towering buildings hid the sun, people were rushing in every direction, and all the open space was covered with concrete. She gave Ben a quick glance to see how he was reacting, and to her amusement his mouth was open like a country bumpkin come to the city for the first time. Jennie decided they would definitely need Dr. Singleton.

The taxi driver spoke broken English but knew their destination and shortly turned into the circular drive of a glass-fronted building with high doors that were constantly revolving. Jennie wondered how they would get through them with their suitcases, but as soon as they were on the sidewalk a uniformed man from the hotel picked up their bags and went ahead of them into the lobby.

Jennie quickly followed after him, then caught her breath. It seemed the builders had brought most of the marble in the world into this lobby, shaping counters, floors, walls, pillars. Huge flower displays graced the open space. Glass tables were covered with magazines where guests were sipping drinks from dainty cups and shaped glasses, attendants at their elbows to serve them.

Dr. Singleton had left her standing alone while he and Ben went to the desk to check in, but the voice that startled her was familiar.

"Miss Reyes?"

Jennie turned to once again be overwhelmed by Riley Singer looking down at her.

"Mr. Singer?" Then without thinking she added, "What are you doing here?"

"If you must know, my favorite witness has crossed state lines, several of them in fact, and my job is to keep track of her." He flashed that beautiful smile, causing Jennie's heart to jump.

"But how did you know where we, er, I was going?"

"That's my job, Miss Reyes. By the way, may I call you Jennie?"

Jennie told herself to get a grip. She felt like a trembling schoolgirl in his presence.
"I don't know why not. It is my name," was her answer, accompanied by an almost coquettish smile.

Ben and Dr. Singleton turned away from the desk just in time to see Jennie's smile. "Ah," said Dr. Singleton, "she is a great beauty."

"That she is, Doctor. But she has several years of school ahead to fulfill her dream of being a medical doctor, so there is no room in her life for a man right now." Ben hoped he spoke the truth, yet Jennie was definitely flirting with Riley.

"Too bad. She would make you a good wife. You don't have one, do you?"

"What?" said a distracted Ben. "Oh, no, I'm still single and looking."

"Ah, you should look her way. Maybe she will look at you like she is looking at the gentleman from the FBI," was Singleton's response.

"How do you know that he's with the FBI?" asked Ben.

"We were told that if she came they would have to follow her. She is a witness in a trial that's coming up, right?" Singleton knew everything about the trial, since it was also his job to make sure the FBI knew where Jennie was during her stay in New York.

When Ben didn't respond, Singleton took the opportunity to guide his guests to their separate rooms, tell them where the restaurants were, and suggest that since they didn't have to report to the convention until the following day, he would be glad to show them a great restaurant followed by a short tour of the city. With that he left them to rest and ready themselves for the remainder of the day.

Jennie had been awed by the lobby, but she almost danced around her suite on the 15$^{th}$ floor overlooking the city, with the Statue of Liberty in the distance. All thoughts of Ben and Riley disappeared with the wonder of discovery. She wished her mother was with her to share in this amazing place.

A knock at the door brought a huge bouquet and a basket of fruit, the first from Riley Singer, and the second from the hotel, with their complements. Jennie wondered why Riley would send her flowers if he was there on business, but she brushed the thought away as she plopped down on the king size bed, munched on an apple, and soon fell asleep.

Dr. Singleton's call woke her with just enough time to dress for dinner and the promised tour of the city. Thus began a whirlwind of events. Her attractiveness as a guest quickly spread, so that she was in demand at small group parties, asked to say "just a few words" at luncheons, interviewed for TV news of the convention, and was rarely available to Ben or Riley Singer.

She did take time to make several calls to her mother to share her excitement, and using the hotel stationery she found in a drawer, wrote a brief letter to Trisha and Samuel describing New York City and this fabulous hotel, and told them she wished they could be with her for this amazing experience.

## 41.

Ben was to be her escort to the award dinner
on the final evening of the convention. Since it was
'white tie' he had rented a tuxedo at the hotel, had
his hair cut, and shined his shoes to a mirror finish.
More than one woman turned to look at the eligible
professor. Still, he was unprepared when Jennie
met him in the lobby.

She had swept her black hair atop her head,
with tendrils brushing against her cheeks and down
the back of her neck. The shimmering pale blue
cocktail dress hugged her figure, her neck wrapped
in the sparkling necklace her mother had sent her,
and the earrings almost touching her shoulders. She
wore little makeup, just a touch of mascara and
lipstick, but she needed nothing else.

Ben was speechless. His feet felt glued to the
floor as his brain was commanding him to move to
her side. Finally he broke lose, offered her his arm,
and grew an inch or two as he proudly escorted her
into the banquet hall. They were seated side by side
at the head table, and Ben was sure that all eyes
were on Jennie. How could they not be?

Jennie spoke after the award was made,
effortlessly and to a standing ovation. Ben received
a short applause for his nomination efforts, which to
him was quite adequate for the opportunity to be
with Jennie, since this was why he had nominated
her in the first place. After dinner she was quickly
surrounded by well-wishers, so that the evening was
over with no separate time for the two of them.

As they walked to the elevators, Riley Singer
approached Jennie and in front of Ben said, "Did
you like the flowers, Jennie?" Ben didn't hear her
reply. He was busy inwardly kicking himself for
not thinking of flowers for Jennie. What a dufus he
was!

Back on the plane the next day Jennie built her wall of earphones, movie, magazines and sleep to keep Ben at bay. She had decided he was quite a nice person, and very good looking, but keeping her focus on med school, there was no room in her life for him or anyone else.

It was hard, however, to keep the image of Riley Singer out of her thoughts. She knew she could be tempted to break her rule for him, and was glad that he would not -- nor Ben either, for that matter –be on campus in her junior year.

## 42.

The summer flew by. Jennie returned to work at the clinic where she had spent the previous summer, helping the physicians wherever she could.

Each weekend she would spend at home with her mother. The two shared stories of Kenya and New York, went to movies, ate popcorn, hiked in the woods. They cherished their time together, knowing that once Jennie was in med school these precious days would disappear. The bond was so strong between them that they could finish each other's sentences. Laughter was frequent, and hugs commonplace.

The letters that arrived every few days from Ben were read by both of them. Jennie told her mother about him, how he always seemed to be in her life, even though she did nothing to encourage him.

"Do you like him, Jennie?" Joan asked quietly one day.

Jennie thought a minute, then replied, "Let's put it this way. I don't exactly not like him. I just don't have room in my life for any man until I'm through med school."

"That's a very long time, Jennie," was Joan's response. "Don't close your heart. You might miss the very person God wants in your life."

"Okay, mom. I'll think about that." Jennie said, and then promptly changed the subject. Her mother was usually right, but probably not this time.

Ben asked to visit during the summer, but Jennie said no, and she didn't show her mother that letter from Ben.

Vacation over, Jennie's junior year moved swiftly while she wrestled with pre-med courses. Others would have thought each class was tough: she found them easy, just what she wanted to study. In fact, they were so simple for her that she had decided to forego the senior year and go straight to medical school. Her exploration efforts while a sophomore had paid off with two tentative offers of admission, one from Harvard in Boston and the other from Johns Hopkins in Baltimore. The trip to New York City had turned her toward the east coast, so now it was a matter of which school would take her without her senior year.

Letters continued to arrive regularly from Ben. Sometimes Jennie left them unopened, but occasionally she would read one and respond with a short note. Sheriton University was a good place for him, and his happiness showed in his letters. He loved the eastern United States and assured her that she would like it also. The cold, snowy winter, his first ever, was exciting to him, allowing him to stay inside and catch up on all the reading he needed to do.

Letters and phone calls also came from Riley Singer with updates on J.W. Williams' forthcoming trial. Jennie heard on the news that there were seventeen drug dealers working with J.W. and all were being held without bail. No mention was made of Callegua's possible involvement, for which Jennie was very glad.

After midterms of the second semester, Alice Dakin and Chris Conrad announced their engagement at the campus Junior-Senior Banquet, with Jennie and the other Kenya team members cheering them on.

Meghan and David kept in touch with emails and pictures attached of baby Monica Letitia in their tiny seminary apartment. David had been accepted at several schools but decided on Princeton because it most agreed with his theological positions and gave him a good student loan package. He had found employment as a youth coordinator in a local church, which gave them a small income, but more importantly the assurance that they would be welcomed by a congregation. Baby Monica was in fact quite a star in the youth group who quickly nicknamed her Letty.

The acceptance letter from Harvard came the same day as Riley Singer's phone call. "Jennie," the familiar voice began, "we have a trial date. July 14th. That means you will soon receive a summons to testify. Do you mind if I come to campus to discuss your appearance in court?"

"Can it wait until Easter break?" was Jennie's calm reply. "You could come to my home instead of campus." She really didn't want her friends to see her with him, knowing that she had resolved to keep away from any romantic attachments. They might get the wrong idea.

"That works for me. You name the date and I'll be there."

After Riley hung up, Jennie called her mother and told her what to expect, making sure her mother knew this was strictly about the trial. Joan was delighted. She had seen how Jennie's eyes lit up when she talked about Riley and now she would get to meet him.

"Oh, and I have great news, mother," Jennie had added at the end of the conversation, "I've been accepted at Harvard Medical School for next year. I hope you won't be too disappointed at my skipping my senior year and graduation."

Joan smiled as she said, "Mind? I expected you to do this from the moment you got your scholarship. I'm proud of you. As the kids around here say, 'You go, girl!'"

The future was looking brighter all the time for Jennie. Once this trial was behind her, it was full steam ahead. In spite of the trial date, she planned to go right into summer classes at Harvard, maybe get on as a research assistant, and still have time to explore the East Coast before winter set in. Her excitement bubbled over in a long letter to Ben, which surprised both of them.

Riley came on Good Friday. The farm fields around Jennie's house were covered with fresh spring growth washed by yesterday's showers. The equipment parked by the two huge barns behind the house spoke of the large farming operation that Joan had built. When Jennie heard his car, she stood in the door to greet him, dressed in jeans and an oversized shirt, her hair pulled back in a ponytail, and her feet shoved into flip flops.

Looking at her and knowing what he had to do, Riley cursed his job and wished for this trial to be over.

They settled at the kitchen table, with coffee and chocolate chip cookies, which happened to be Riley's favorite. Joan liked this man. He would make a good match for Jennie, probably better than the professor who kept pursuing her. Jennie was thinking the same thing.

"Jennie, Mrs. Reyes," Riley began, "what I'm about to tell you is something you don't want to hear. So after I've told you, please wait a few minutes before you respond, okay?"

They nodded their heads and waited for him to continue.

Riley squirmed in his chair. He didn't want to do this, but it had to be. "Jennie, we – my supervisors and I – have decided you have to go into hiding." He hurried on, words tumbling without making sense in Jennie's mind that was screaming no, no, no. "We have discovered that the word is out that you are the only one who witnessed the trade at the airport, and you are being targeted by affiliates of the drug dealers we're holding in prison." There. He'd said it.

"What…. what do you mean, targeted?" Jennie's world was collapsing. Surely this couldn't be true.

"They mean to kill you so you can't witness. With Sue dead, and the only other witness J.W.'s son who could be a biased witness because he's a family member, you are the key to J.W.'s arrest. The FBI tracked his deals and dealers, but the arrest was dependent on the actual trade at the airport. There's a contract out on you. You are in real danger."

"But…. but…med school. What about it? I'm supposed to start in a couple of months. Everything is set. Don't you understand? I've been accepted to Harvard from my junior year. Not many students get that opportunity. And I'm on a full scholarship. And you're telling me I have to go into hiding?" Jennie reached for her mother's hand. It was cold and moist as Joan's heart was reacting to what had befallen her daughter.

"Med school will have to wait. We will change your name. You'll need to change your appearance. Maybe die your hair and cut it. We'll give you a secure apartment and you'll have a security officer near you at all times. And this has to happen immediately."

"But I have to finish the semester," Jennie exclaimed.

"We've thought about that. Your instructors have agreed to send your required work to you via an FBI contact so that you can finish the year. After that, we can't promise anything."

Tears ran down Joan's face. All of Jennie's plans and dreams were crashing onto the kitchen floor. She realized that even she would not be allowed to have contact with Jennie, her only family. The kitchen began to whirl around her. The pain in her chest...

"Mother? Mother, are you all right?" Jennie finally came into focus.

Joan realized she was lying in a bed, a hospital bed. How did she get here? "Jennie? Is that you?" She wasn't sure if this was Jennie. Her short blonde hair, thin eyebrows, and heavy makeup changed her altogether.

"Hurry up, miss," a male voice said. "We've got to get you out of here."

"Mother, you'll be fine. You didn't have a heart attack. It was just a TIA and you'll go home tomorrow. A woman from our church will take care of you for a few days. But I have to leave. They're taking me into hiding. If you want to know anything, call Mr. Singer. He will know where I am. I love you, mother. You know I do." Jennie bent over and kissed her mother. Hoping it was true, she added, "We'll find a way to be in touch."

## 43.

As Jennie left the room to join the security

guard, she slapped on a pair of large, horn-rimmed glasses. The transformation from Jennie to Rita Sanchez, her new name, was almost complete.

The following day Riley Singer met with President Ingram at Callegua, and explained to him the situation that Jennie was in. They agreed that her professors would bring her class work each week to the President's office, where Riley would pick it up, then return Jennie's finished papers and tests. Fortunately, there were just a few weeks left until the end of the semester, and since Jennie was an excellent student, her professors were willing to go along with the arrangement.

To explain the need for this extraordinary plan, they were told that Jennie had been tapped to participate in a government program which she had to start immediately. This was also the answer given to students concerned about Jennie's sudden disappearance. The "buzz" died down in a couple of weeks and Callegua went on as usual.

At Sheriton University, Dr. Ben started to receive returned letters he had mailed to Jennie that were stamped "Not at this address." Alarmed, he sent letters to her home and these were returned marked "unknown". When he tried to call, the phones were "no longer in service." The phone information service was no help. "No one by that name" was the answer he got back, both for Jennie and her mother Joan. Finally, desperate, he contacted Callegua University's president whose secretary gave them the standard answer: Jennie had been tapped for a government program, and no, they had no contact information. Ben stared at the phone. He was relieved to know that she was alive, but he was at a dead end in his search.

"Just a moment," the secretary said, "perhaps you should talk to President Ingram." She knew

Ben as their former history professor and wanted to help him.

After a few moments, Ingram came on the line. "Ben? How are you? How's Sheriton?"

Ben gave him a perfunctory answer, then added, "You remember the student, Jennie Reyes, who won the history scholarship? I really need to contact her, but she seems to have disappeared off the face of the planet. Can you give me any help?"

Ingram was quiet a moment, then said, "Well, maybe I can help. If you want to send a letter for her to my office, I might be able to get it to her. Address an outer envelope to me marked personal, and put her letter in a sealed envelope inside. No promises though. I don't know where she is and I'm not sure it will work. But we can give it a try. And, Ben, if it is picked up, I can't promise that it won't be opened, maybe even censored. That's a chance you'll have to take."

Ben thanked President Ingram profusely, added a few sentences about Sheriton as compared to Callegua, expressed again his appreciation, and hung up. No promises, he mused. What on earth was Jennie involved in? He immediately sat down at his desk and began to write.

In Iowa, the FBI asked Joan to put a supervisor in charge of her farming operation and quietly move to a small town several hundred miles away. There she was to use an assumed name in keeping with a new social security card, driver's license, and insurance. Her business dealings with the supervisor were carried out by the new registered owner of her farm, an FBI officer, so that she would not be traced. She was not in direct danger, but could be if someone wanted to attack her to get to Jennie.

As for Jennie, Riley scarcely knew her when

he next saw her. Short blond hair, glasses, heavy makeup, and clothes worthy of a streetwalker. No one would take her for the black-haired beauty that had begun to catch his affections.

"Jennie," he had said, "I'm so sorry you have to do this. Really, I am. And I promise you, I'll find a way for you to go to med school. Maybe not Harvard, but somewhere. One day this will be over, and you will be a doctor. I promise."

She turned away from him. Jennie was sure that not even Riley Singer could make med school happen. Her life was over before it had begun. She had decided that even God had deserted her. She would never live a normal life again. At least she had her class work to concentrate on. For now it would have to be her salvation.

## 44.

The tiny apartment that was Jennie's prison soon filled with medical books, as she spent her time absorbing all the knowledge she could. Anything she needed was brought to her, so that by the time July 14th arrived, she was almost literally climbing the walls, she so wanted to get outside. Riley had promised that once her testimony was over, they would move her to a place where she would have more freedom.

Each morning Jennie eagerly read the newspaper that was left outside her door. On the 14th the Williams trial story was buried in the back of the front section. The article was brief and almost hidden at the bottom of a page. Obviously the FBI did not want the attention that a major story would have, which Jennie found curious. When Riley called that afternoon, she asked him about it.

"We have more dealers to arrest, Jennie," Riley answered. "This operation was a lot larger than we thought. The Africa connection by itself is continent wide. We didn't know that when we arrested Williams." He paused, then added, "I don't want to get your hopes up, but we may have a new development that will let you off the hook."

Jenny gasped. "What? What is it?"

"Can't tell you yet, but as soon as it's a sure thing, I'll let you know." Then Riley added, "Oh, by the way, that history professor who got you the scholarship has been pressing me. He really wants to see you. Are you interested if I can arrange it?"

Jennie glanced at the stack of letters sitting on her desk, all from Ben Adkins. They had been her one touch of normalcy, an eye to the outside world while she lived inside. He had become her friend. When her class work had arrived, a letter from Ben was usually in the package, and she missed it when it wasn't there. A time or two she had gone on a frantic search of all the books and papers in the package, and even wept when there was no letter.

As she was about to answer Riley, she happened to catch her image in the mirror by the door. Ben should never see her like this, this ugly blond hair, the makeup, the glasses. He probably would not even know her.

To Riley she said, "Maybe after the trial is over, but not now. Thanks anyway."

She wasn't called to testify until the middle of August. Riley had spent the previous two days with her, going over the kind of questions she might be asked. When the time came for her testimony she was escorted to the courtroom under heavy guard, with Riley making sure her face was covered with a semi-shear scarf to shield her from the news cameras.

During the weeks that the trial had progressed, so had the media presence, especially after the scope of arrests became known. This week the

judge had ordered the court room cleared of all
visitors, so that the three young people who would
be called to witness could have privacy.

On entering the room Jennie immediately
recognized Doug Williams and figured that the
young woman beside him was Laina, his sister.
Riley whispered to her that they had both testified
the day before, that they were there at the request of
the Judge, and that the cross examination from
Williams' lawyers had been intense, pointing out
that they were testifying against their Father. In
fact, Laina, in tears, had told what a wonderful
parent he had been, always providing the best of
everything for the family. Even Doug's witness
seemed reasonably suspect since he said he was
simply doing a favor for his Dad by picking up the
valise at the airport in Kenya, a story that any son
could make up.

Judge Baker had not wanted this case. He
was nearing retirement and had asked to be assigned
to short, uncomplicated cases that would not drag
over into his retirement date. However, he had
litigated several major drug cases, and he had been
scheduled for this trial. It was in his best interest to
see that the case move swiftly.

Shortly after Judge Baker had entered the
courtroom and they had all been seated, Jennie was
called to the witness stand and sworn in. Her face
was still covered and the judge asked her to remove
the scarf. The Prosecuting Attorney requested that
it remain to protect her identity, since they had
learned that a contract had been put out on her.

"Do you know anyone in this courtroom?" he
asked Jennie, nee Rita Sanchez.

"Yes, your honor, I do," was her reply.

"And who might that be? Name them, and
point them out, please."

Jennie pointed out Doug and said, "Doug Williams."

"Can you point out J.W. Williams also?"

"Well, I have never met him, but that man," Jennie said, pointing at J.W., "is the one I saw Doug Williams give a valise to."

"You may leave the scarf on, Miss Sanchez." Turning to the prosecution, Judge Baker said, "Your witness." He had satisfied himself that she was a valid witness, and judging from what he knew about J.W. Williams, that J.W. was probably a part of the contract to kill Jennie.

Several questions later, after Jennie had told about the trip to Kenya with Doug as travel agent, her knowledge of J.W.'s wife Sue, the mission run by Trisha, and her own desired career as a medical doctor, having planned to go to med school from her junior year at Callegua University until this trial had interrupted her life, the Defense Attorney began to question her.

She held steadfastly to her testimony, just as Riley expected her to do. She defended Doug's innocence, told how naïve he had been on the plane, how he trusted his father, only to discover he had been set up. The Defense Attorney was no match for Jennie's truthful answers and quick mind.

Finally the judge cut off the cross-examination, remonstrating the attorney that he had given him more than enough time without any progress.

"Is there anything more that needs to be said to or about this witness?" Judge Baker was clearly exasperated at the time the defense attorney had taken.

"Yes, your honor. The FBI wishes to put into evidence this enhanced video taken from the airport security camera. On it is the clear picture of Doug

Williams greeting his father and handing the valise
to him, this man, J.W. Williams." He pointed across
the room. "If Miss Sanchez had never testified, it
would not matter. The camera is its own witness."

Jennie was dismissed. As she was escorted
out of the courtroom, face still covered, surrounded
by security guards, she began to realize what had
just happened. They hadn't needed her witness
after all, except to clear her of any involvement.
The video must have been what Riley referred to
when he said there was a development that might let
her off the hook. It was the video that condemned
J.W., not her testimony.

She had seen J.W. slump down in his seat,
defeat written on his face, and she remembered her
mother's description of the student council trial at
Callegua when J.W. set up Sue to take the rap for
him, just like now he had hoped to pin the blame on
Doug, his son.

Jennie was hurried past the cameras. When
she arrived at her apartment, Riley was waiting for
her.

"Jennie, as a safeguard we think you ought to
stay here another month, just like you are. Then, if
the drug dealers have realized that the video is the
convicting piece of evidence, we think they will
forget about you. But just in case, we have
arranged for Harvard to admit you under Rita
Sanchez. Keep your hair blond and your glasses on,
and we think you can hide, as we say, 'in plain
sight'. in medical school."

Jennie threw her arms around Riley.

"Oh thank you, thank you, thank you!" Then
remembering, she asked, "What about my mother?"

"We're going to let her go back about the
same time. The supervising foreman has done a
good job. The crops were planted on time, the
disking and fertilizing—everything has gone as

planned through our contacts between him and your mother. She will come home to an excellent operation running just as smoothly as ever."

Jennie flopped down into a chair, exhaustion running out of her fingertips. "I don't know what to say, except I am just so grateful to you, Riley. Without you I would never have gotten through this horror." Then looking into space, she added quietly, "I guess God didn't desert me after all."

Riley rose to leave. At the door he paused, reached into his inside pocket, and drew out a thick letter.

"I almost forgot. Dr. Adkins sent this letter to me for you, after I told him you didn't want to see him until after you had testified. I suggest you read it. He has been almost frantic not knowing where you were."

Riley handed the letter to Jennie, and added, "It's been great working with you, Jennie. After you've read the letter, if you want to see Dr. Adkins, just let me know," and he made his exit.

Riley had figured out that as much as he liked Jennie, Ben loved her. He wasn't going to stand in the way of a love like that. Besides, the woman he married should be just a bit more submissive than Jennie would ever be. An FBI agent and a medical doctor? He just didn't think so.

## 45.

Jennie was exhausted from the day's events. As soon as Riley was gone, she curled up in the one comfortable chair in her apartment, pulled a throw blanket over her, and promptly fell asleep. It was dark outside when she was wakened by hunger.

The refrigerator was well stocked, and she soon had a sandwich made, a bag of chips, and a cup of hot chocolate. The TV beckoned, but a crinkly sound under her reminded her of Ben's letter. She set down her plate to open the letter, smoothed out the three pages covered with Ben's familiar handwriting, and began to read. Her food was forgotten after the first sentence...

My dearest Jennie,

I hope you will not be offended by what I will say in this letter, but I can no longer wait to say it.

I love you, Jennie. I have loved you from the first day I set eyes on you in the front row of my history class. You may not have noticed, but the first thing I did when class was to begin was to see if you were there.

Your beauty captivated me, but I was bound by faculty rules, so I "accidentally" would appear somewhere close to you in ways that no one would notice. You noticed, and even if you rejected me, I kept trying. I wanted to know you; I wanted to hold you. I want to marry you, and I have since that first day.

When I moved to Sheriton I dreamed of dating you this summer, of convincing you of my love, of holding you in my arms and kissing your perfect lips.

Instead, you disappeared. Frantic, I searched everywhere to find you. My letters to you were returned 'not at this address' or 'unknown'. Letters I sent to your home were returned, and both your campus and home phones were out of service, discontinued.

Finally I called President Ingram at Callegua, whose secretary told me you have been tapped for a government program. Ingram hesitantly decided to let my letters through, along with your class work.

Lest you reject the letters, I never let you know how devastated I was, how I longed for you. When you mentioned Riley Singer in one of your letters, I contacted him immediately. He assured me that you were all right, but could not be seen by anyone, at least until the end of July.

Jennie, my Jennie, my love, July is almost over, and thank God, Mr. Singer is carrying this letter to you. I begged him to let me come to you, but he said that would happen only if you allowed me to come.

Please, Jennie. I don't know where you have been or what you have been doing, but just to look at you, even once, will take away the great pain in my heart that grows greater each day we are apart. Please let me come to you.

Let me take you in my arms and tell you how much I love you, let me stroke your beautiful hair, taste your wonderful lips. I love you, Jennie, and I want to spend my life with you.

But right now, I just want to see you. Please.

Ben"

The sandwich sat forgotten as Jennie read the letter again and again, almost in a daze. Finally she picked up the phone, called Riley, and said,

"Riley, let Ben come, but be sure you tell him what I look like."

She didn't get much sleep that night. Several times she got up and reread the letter until she had it almost memorized. She understood now why Ben kept showing up close to her on campus, and to think she was ready to charge him with harassment...

Riley called around ten a.m. "Jennie, I got your call last night, and relayed your ok to Ben. Even as we speak he is on a plane coming here. Of course, our security people will check him out, and extra guards will be close by in case something goes wrong." He paused, then added, "Enjoy the visit. You may not get another one very soon."

Jennie hated the way she looked, the short, icky blond hair especially, but Ben would have to accept this...and she knew he would. She guessed Ben would come about three o'clock. What to wear? She only had ugly, ill-fitting clothes; nothing very pretty. Choosing the least offensive blouse and her jeans, she found her excitement growing as she showered and dressed. In fact, she surprised herself by singing a little song with one word: "Ben".

And then she sat down to wait. Turning on the TV she was startled to see Samuel being interviewed by a reporter, something about the mission, but it was the end of the interview and she didn't know what he had said. It was great to see him, she decided, and probably something important had happened at the mission.

At noon she took yesterday's sandwich out of the frig and ate it without tasting it. Her emotions were completely messed up, and for once Jennie didn't want to put everything straight in her mind. Ben would let her go to med school...after all, he got the scholarship for her. And maybe a professor was a good partner for a doctor.

Jennie's mind ran as she watched the clock move slowly, ever so slowly, until it reached three o'clock. Three fifteen. Three thirty. Jennie began to pace back and forth in her tiny apartment. She checked the phone to see if it was working and heard a steady dial tone. As the time inched toward four she began to be alarmed. What if the FBI wouldn't let him come? Maybe he failed their clearance...

She was so distraught that she didn't hear the steps in the hall, or the key turn in the lock. Suddenly he was there, tall, good looking, his hair dropped over his forehead. He was looking at her quizzically.

"Jennie? My blond Jennie?"

She answered with a nervous laugh. "It's me, Ben." And then she was in his arms, his lips were on hers.

"Jennie, I love you. I love you. I love you! Do you think you can ever love me?"

"Oh, Ben, I think I already do." Ben kissed her again. At last she was his. A shiver of joy swept over him. Jennie nestled closer to him, surrounded by his strong arms, and instantly knew that with Ben she would always be loved, she would always be safe.

One day Dr. Ben and Dr. Jennie would look back on this moment and decide that it was the most special afternoon of their lives.

Ever.

## Epilogue

**From the Daily Nation\***
Nairobi, Kenya, 1997

**KENYA MISSION GONE**
By Samuel Katata

Rebels moved through the
countryside last week, burning
and killing. At the orphanage
founded over 20 years ago by
Trisha McClellan, the children,
workers, and Miss McClellan
were locked in the main school
room which was then burned
to the ground, killing all. The
storeroom was emptied, then
it and all other buildings were
burned.

This reporter once worked at
the orphanage and had the
highest respect for the work
done to aid children orphaned
by AIDS and related diseases.
No one has been arrested for
this crime against Kenya's
children.

**From the Chicago
Sun-Times, 1997***

**CALLEGUA U GIFT**

Callegua University President John Ingram today
announced an undesignated
gift of almost $2 million
from the estate of Trisha
McClellan, a 1976 graduate,
whose orphanagein Kenya
was destroyed by rebels
last month. In the event
of such a happening,
McClellan had named
Callegua University as sole
beneficiary of the funds
previously given to the
orphanage by former CU
student Sue Pendella.
President Ingram said
the University Trustees
would determine the best
use of the money at their
July meeting.

*fictional

The story continues in the forthcoming book:
**The Professor's Obsessions
What Would Jake Do?**
*The 2010's*

*~Publisher's Invitation~*

*As publisher of the nonprofit Preservation Foundation I invite you to visit us at our website. While there you can read some of our 1,000 plus stories, enter one of our annual nonfiction writing contests, or find out how we can help you publish your own book.*

*If you wish to purchase more copies of this book you can buy it from Ruth at her website-- www.ruthtruman.com*

*It is also available from Amazon and many other fine booksellers.*

*I hope you'll visit us soon.*

*Richard Loller*

*The Preservation Foundation, Inc.*
*www.storyhouse.org*
*preserve@storyhouse.org*
*615 889-2968*

*Preserving the extraordinary stories of 'ordinary' people*

Made in the USA
San Bernardino, CA
25 June 2019